TOM SWIFT™

young inventor

Don't miss any of Tom's adventures!

TOM SWIFT™
young inventor

#2

THE ROBOT OLYMPICS

By Victor Appleton

Aladdin Paperbacks
New York London Toronto Sydney

This book is a work of fiction. Any references to historical events,
real people, or real locales are used fictitiously. Other names,
characters, places, and incidents are the product of the author's
imagination, and any resemblance to actual events or locales or
persons, living or dead, is entirely coincidental.

ALADDIN PAPERBACKS
An imprint of Simon & Schuster Children's Publishing Division
1230 Avenue of the Americas, New York, NY 10020
Copyright © 2006 by Simon & Schuster Inc.

All rights reserved, including the right of
reproduction in whole or in part in any form.
ALADDIN PAPERBACKS and colophon are trademarks of
Simon & Schuster, Inc.
Designed by Lisa Vega
The text of this book was set in Weiss.
Manufactured in the United States of America
First Aladdin Paperbacks edition June 2006
2 4 6 8 10 9 7 5 3 1

Library of Congress Control Number 2005937379
ISBN-13: 978-1-4169-1361-0
ISBN-10: 1-4169-1361-0

Contents

One-on-One

"Score!"

The basketball swished through the net as my sneakers slapped down onto the hardwood floor. A perfect slam dunk! I turned to face my opponent.

SwiftBot-1 gleamed beneath the LED lights overhead. His silver-metallic body was about my height, roughly five feet ten inches, and mimicked your basic humanoid design: two arms, two legs, one head, and so on. Jointed arms gave him a standing reach of over seven feet. Inside his lightweight, carbon-fiber exterior was an array of integrated circuits, servos, optical sensors, wires, and batteries. His smiling steel face was just for show, except for the pair of glowing infrared sensors that served as his eyes.

I thought he looked pretty impressive, but, of course, I was biased. I had built SwiftBot myself, with plenty of help from my friends.

I saw my face reflected in his polished silver torso. Blue eyes. Blond hair. A backward baseball cap kept sweat from dripping into my eyes. My face was flushed from the exercise.

"Your ball." I tossed the bright orange sphere over to SwiftBot-1, which caught it with both hands. This part of my private lab had been converted into a half-court playing area for testing the robot's hoop skills one-on-one. "Play offense."

Voice-recognition software let him respond to my verbal command. He dribbled the ball against the floor, keeping it close to his body for better control. Titanium-alloy muscles flexed smoothly as he went into action. *Looks good*, I thought, nodding in approval. Teaching a robot to dribble hadn't been easy. My friend Yolanda and I had spent hours trying to get the programming and mechanics right.

In a way I was sort of playing against myself. Tom Swift, amateur athlete, versus Tom Swift, teenage inventor. And the inventor in me was definitely rooting for the robot.

SwiftBot charged toward the free-throw lane while I scooted to keep between him and the hoop. Pausing right at the edge of the paint, he went into the classic triple-threat stance: feet spread, knees apart, elbows in. Like a human athlete, SwiftBot could either shoot, pass, or dribble from this posture. Of course, with no one to pass to in this one-on-one match, the robot's options were reduced to either dribbling or taking a shot. I couldn't wait to see what he'd do next.

Yo had programmed SwiftBot to vary its behavior, so that his play wouldn't become too predictable. Right now, I knew, the microprocessors in his electronic brain were analyzing the data from its sensors in order to rapidly arrive at a decision. His sculpted face offered no hint as to what he was thinking. Talk about a poker face! It occurred to me that a robot card shark would have a distinct advantage over a human player.

Hmm. Might be an interesting project for the future . . .

SwiftBot's head swiveled from left to right and

back, trying to fake me out, but I spotted his legs bending at the knee joints and guessed that he was going for a jump shot. I gave him props for trying to bluff me, though, and wondered if his move would have fooled another robot.

Guess we'll find out soon.

Sure enough, SwiftBot went airborne the next second. Foam rubber springs in the soles of his feet gave him extra lift as he pushed off the floor. Metallic fingers held the ball poised above his head, ready to go. At the very top of his jump, SwiftBot released the ball from his fingers. He was going for it!

I jumped, too, hoping to block his shot, but he had too much altitude on me. For a second, I kicked myself for making his arms so long. Eyes wide, I watched the ball arc over my head, just beyond my fingertips. SwiftBot had calculated its trajectory perfectly. The ball passed right through the hoop without even grazing the rim.

One point to SwiftBot!

He landed easily back onto the floor, the springs in his feet doubling as shock absorbers. I was stoked to see him stick the landing so well. The first couple of times we'd played against each other, he had lost his balance after every other jump. I winced at the memory of SwiftBot toppling over onto the floor. He still had trouble getting up if he landed flat on his back, but, thanks to a new-and-improved internal gyroscope, he didn't fall down as much anymore, thank goodness. I was tired of hammering out the dents in his outer casing.

"Way to go!" I congratulated him. The score was now 10-6 in my favor. Not bad for a robot who had been playing b-ball for only a couple of months now. Still, my inner inventor couldn't help but wish that he was winning.

That would be seriously cool.

SwiftBot said nothing in reply. No big surprise there since his mouth was strictly decorative. It had been tempting to install a speaker so that he could talk back, but that would have required additional software as well. We sacrificed speech to devote more memory to his motor skills.

"Okay," I said, reclaiming the ball. One more point and I would win the match. "Play defense."

SwiftBot took up a defensive position just outside the post. Infrared sensors scanned my every movement.

Dribbling the ball against the floor, I darted to the right of the free-throw lane. The sound of the orange leather ball bouncing against the hardwood echoed throughout the lab. Adrenalin rushed through my veins as I rushed toward the low post, keeping my eyes on the hoop. My own sneakers were equipped with sensors, microchips, and a motor and cabling system that allowed the shoes to adjust to my gait on the fly. I felt like I was running on air.

SwiftBot matched my moves with his own. He kept between me and the hoop, extending his arms and elbows out to the side to take up as much space as possible. The flexible joints in his knees bent slightly in anticipation of a jump.

I didn't even try to fake him out. My brain already had way more computing power than his, so it seemed unfair to pull any mind games on him. Instead I decided to rely on my own natural speed and agility. Maybe SwiftBot could jump higher than I could, but I had faster reflexes.

The higher I dribbled, the quicker I could move, so I really let the ball bounce as I sprinted to the left of SwiftBot and took my shot. I put a bit of backspin on the ball as it left my fingers, wishing for the hundredth time that I could engineer a way for SwiftBot to do the same. That was just too subtle a move for the robot's mechanical fingers to master, however. His tactile sensors weren't that precise.

Maybe for SwiftBot-2 . . .

I held my breath as I watched the ball soar toward the hoop. If I sunk this shot, the game was over.

But SwiftBot wasn't beaten yet. My heart leaped as the robot sprang into the air at a forty-five-degree angle. His right arm stretched out above his head, intercepting the spinning ball in midair. Leather smacked against a carbon-fiber palm as SwiftBot batted the ball back at me.

"Wow!" I exclaimed. "Pretty slick!"

Caught by surprise, I almost let the ball bounce out of bounds. The unmistakable *ba-boom-ba* of a loose basketball called out to me and I raced after the air-filled sphere like a maniac. My hands grabbed onto the ball at the last minute, and I spun back toward the hoop.

To my relief SwiftBot was still on his feet, despite leaping diagonally after the ball. He wobbled on one leg for a moment, struggling to regain his balance, then landed both feet on the floor. *Smooth move*, I thought, mentally cheering him on. I could win easily if he fell over, but that was the last thing I wanted. The better SwiftBot played, the more it felt like a victory.

But that didn't mean I was going to make it too easy on him.

Taking advantage of my human speed, I dashed around SwiftBot, dribbling the ball with my right hand. My plan was to make a close-range shot on the run before the robot could get into position to block me again. I scrambled toward the hoop until I was only about six feet from the basket. Without coming to a halt, I lifted off on my left foot and with my right hand aimed for the upper-right corner of the white targeting box painted on the clear SwiftGlass back-board. My eyes tracked the ball as I dropped toward the floor. Had I made the layup?

Too late to stop my shot, SwiftBot rushed in front of me, hoping to snag the rebound just in case my shot missed. His metal arms shot up to box me out.

It was good strategy, but a wasted effort in this case. The ball hit the backboard right where it was supposed to. With a resounding boom, the ball banked off the SwiftGlass into the net. *Swish!*

"Game over," I announced, but SwiftBot's computerized brain had already calculated the score as well. His arms dropped to his sides and he came to halt. He knew that my eleven points meant that I had won the match. Fortunately, Yo had programmed him to be a good loser.

No robot of mine was going to go on a Terminator-like rampage. That only happened in the movies.

SwiftBot stood quietly upon the court. If nothing else, he looked less tired than I felt. Breathing hard, I retrieved the ball and strolled over to the sideline, where I dropped down onto a bench. A bottle of cold water was waiting for me, and I gulped down the liquid eagerly. SwiftBot didn't have to worry about getting dehydrated, but I did.

I glanced up at video cameras mounted above and around the court. The whole match had been digitally recorded so that Yo and I could analyze Swift-Bot's performance later. I made a mental note to e-mail the footage to Yo right away. She'd want to pick apart the robot's moves frame by frame.

In the meantime, I ran over the game in my head. Today's 11-6 was SwiftBot's best score to date. It was a bummer to keep beating him all the time, but I reminded myself that his real competition was other robots. If he could do this well against an actual human being, he was sure to keep winning against his fellow machines—or so I hoped.

His reflexes were still a little slower than I liked. Maybe if I squeezed a few more microprocessors into his neural network . . . ?

Before I could pursue the idea any further, a familiar voice interrupted my thoughts. "Hey, dawg!" my wristwatch blurted. "Better get a move on. You're going to be late for dinner."

The voice belonged to Q.U.I.P., short for Quantum Utilizing Interactive Processor, an artificial intelligence that was basically the world's smartest PDA. A chip in my wristwatch connected me with the powerful servers and supercomputer running Q.U.I.P.'s software. The AI had been up and running for only about a year now, but already I had no idea how I had ever coped without him. It was like having a backup brain.

"Thanks for the alert!" I said. Playing against

10

SwiftBot, I had completely lost track of the time, but now that I actually looked at my watch I saw that it was almost seven. A growl from my stomach confirmed that I was running late for dinner. "Tell my folks I'll be right there." Q.U.I.P. was set up to interface with the rest of the household computers and systems. "Oh yeah, and e-mail the latest b-ball training footage to Yolanda. Triple encrypted, please."

"No problemo," the AI assured me. I was proud that Q.U.I.P. didn't talk like a stereotypical movie computer. None of that "insufficient data . . . cannot compute" baloney. Right now I had him set on Standard American Teen, but I could change his voice and speech patterns as easily as I could download a new ring tone for my cell phone. After *Pirates of the Caribbean* came out, I had him talking like a buccaneer for a week, just for the fun of it. "I've got your back, man."

"You know it," I said.

With no time to lose, I instructed SwiftBot to recharge his batteries, then left the robot training room. The rest of my laboratory filled up a blast-proof concrete bunker that was buried deep into a hill behind our house, a safe distance away from my family's actual living quarters. (Hey, accidents happen!) Various tools and instruments cluttered the stainless steel counters in the workshop area, and a mounted fume hood provided adequate ventilation for working with noxious chemicals. The assorted equipment included a laser wielder, a miniature cyclotron, an electron microscope, and even a rapid prototyping machine that could make usable components out of plastic powder. Among various half-finished projects, put aside while I focused on SwiftBot, was a zero-gravity jetpack. Modular partitions allowed me to rearrange the layout of the lab as needed.

The overhead lights switched off automatically as I left the lab. An air-lock door slammed shut behind me. Only I knew the password to open the air lock, although my parents always had the option of activating an emergency override. I knew SwiftBot would be safe in my absence, no matter how much certain parties might like to get an advance peek at his wiring.

His moment of truth was coming up. Just wait until people saw him in action!

An underground tunnel connected my lab to the house, about five hundred feet away. I stepped onto a moving conveyor belt. My watch chirped again, but this time it wasn't Q.U.I.P.

"Tom?" my mom's voice addressed me. "What's keeping you?"

"I'm on my way!" I promised. "Just give me a second!"

I was sorry to keep everyone waiting, but, hey, I had the Robot Olympics to win.

Tomorrow's Dinner Today

People visiting our home often feel like they've stepped through a time portal into the future. From the outside the house blends in with its neighbors: It *looks* like a traditional Victorian home with a slate roof and red brick walls. Brick-colored ceramic tiles actually cover the outer walls, however, and the dark slate shingles are also made of synthetic tiles that absorb solar energy through super-efficient photovoltaic cells. The house's deceptively old-fashioned facade pulls in enough sunlight to power all the systems inside, even though we have a couple of backup generators to pick up any slack. One of those generators is hooked up to my lab, just in case I need a little extra juice sometimes.

Once you step through the front door, the house stops pretending to be ordinary. There's no such thing as a time machine, but our home is definitely ahead of its time. My dad runs Swift Enterprises, one of the top research and development companies in the world, and he's big into beta testing SE's new inventions at home before marketing them to the general public. As a result every network and appliance in our house is state-of-the-art.

And then some.

The tunnel from my lab leads to our basement. A clear plastic door slid open in front of me, and I hopped off the conveyor belt. Passing the virtual-reality gym in the basement, I ran up the stairs to the ground floor. An automated laundry room is located at the top of the steps, and I took a second to trade my sweaty jersey for a clean T-shirt. I could use a shower, too, but that could wait until later. Hunger took priority over hygiene.

Not quite as stinky, I headed for the dining room. Soothing images of fluffy, white clouds drifted across the "smart" plastic walls, which could be either transparent or opaque, depending on the circumstances. Classical music played softly in the background, and I recognized my mom's favorite evening environmental program. I would have preferred rock-'n'-roll and exploding starbursts myself, but that's why I had my own room. Mom's classical selections were basically "music to digest by."

Motorized cleaning robots, resembling foot-long silver Frisbees, patrolled the carpet and furniture, sucking up dust and dirt. They hummed to each other as they worked, communicating by infrared signals. Possessed of a swarmlike collective intelligence, they operated without human supervision. They expertly dodged my feet as I hustled toward the dining room.

Familiar voices reached my ears. A delicious smell teased my nostrils, making my mouth water. Playing b-ball with SwiftBot had definitely worked up my appetite. *Wonder what's for dinner?*

"Thomas Swift Junior!" Mom exclaimed as I stepped into the dining room. "Look at you. You're a sweaty mess!"

She and Dad and my sister, Sandy, were already seated around the circular dining-room table. An interactive communications console rose from the center of the table. Text and images appeared on the curved plastic screen running all the way around the cylindrical console. At the moment my dad was perusing the nightly news bulletins on the segment of the screen facing his chair. I caught a glimpse of one of the headlines: TERRORIST GROUP DENOUNCES ROBO OLYMPICS.

That didn't sound good.

"Sorry, Mom." I dropped into a nanoplastic chair that automatically fitted itself to the natural contours of my body. "You should have seen me a few minutes ago."

"I can just imagine," she said dryly. Although in her early fifties, she looked at least ten years younger, with short auburn hair and green eyes. Her rumpled flannel shirt and jeans told me she had been working in her studio all day. She shrugged her shoulders, not too upset by my untidy appearance. "At least you're getting plenty of exercise. I can't complain about that."

"Trust me, I got quite a workout just now." I greeted the rest of my family. "Hi, Dad, Sandy."

"Hello, son." Dad continued to scan the news reports. His short blond hair was streaked with gray. A wrinkled brow gave away his age, but, like Mom, he had chosen laser surgery over glasses. People say Sandy and I got our blond hair and blue eyes from him, which I guess made us walking proof that genetics were all they were cracked up to be. A lightweight tweed jacket was draped over the back of his chair. "Glad you could make it."

"Uh-huh, hi," Sandy murmured, distracted. She was busy text-messaging someone—probably her best friend, Philly—via a combination wristwatch and PDA. Sandy's fifteen years old, one year younger than I am, and is only a pain some of the time, as sisters go. She fired off her IM, then eagerly read Philly's response. Her eyes widened in surprise at some unexpected tidbit of news. "No kidding?" she exclaimed out loud. "Get out of here!"

Mom shot Sandy a glance. "Tell Philly you've got to sign off. No instant-messaging at dinner, remember?" My mother swept her gaze over Dad and me, as well. "That goes for the rest of you, too. You know the drill. No e-mail, IMs, phone calls, Web surfing, virtual-reality role-playing, et cetera during meals."

"Understood," Dad said. He pressed a button on the underside of the table and the communications console sunk out of sight, disappearing beneath the surface of the table. Sandy switched off her wrist unit, and I hit the "Do Not Disturb" button on my interface with Q.U.I.P. The artificial intelligence would hold my calls, except for absolute emergencies.

Fine with me, I thought. At the moment, I was craving food, not info. Bites instead of bytes.

A large assortment of fresh sushi was laid out on the table, along with a salad and a pitcher of fruit punch. *Of course*, I thought, finally identifying the mouth-watering aroma that had lured me to the dining room. Dad had picked up "Sozomu," a computerized sushi maker on his last business trip to Tokyo and had been dying to try it out for days. I was all for giving it a test run myself. My hungry stomach felt like it could consume an ocean's worth of raw fish and seaweed.

I helped myself to a salmon roll.

"So how was your day, Mary?" Dad asked my mom. He must have gotten home from work while I was facing off against SwiftBot in the lab. His office upstairs allowed him to work from home most of the time, but occasionally he still had to trek over to SE headquarters, on the outskirts of town. "You making progress on that new figure?"

My mom's a pretty famous sculptor whose wildlife pieces are displayed in galleries all over the world. Mary Nestor Swift is as big a deal in the art world as my dad is in the scientific community.

"I think so," she replied. Bits of reddish clay were embedded beneath her fingertips. Even though she had her own private studio over the garage, the clay always managed to find its way into the rest of the house. The smeary residue kept the cleaning 'bots busy full-time. "The hawk sculpture is almost finished, though I'm going blind doing the detail work on all those feathers." She shook her head and laughed. "Whose idea was it to give birds feathers anyway?"

"Don't look at me," Dad joked. "My inventions are strictly featherless."

Changing the subject, Mom looked across the table at me. "So, tomorrow's the big day, right? You and SwiftBot ready to go?"

"You bet," I answered. Tomorrow marked the beginning of the national finals of the first official Robot Olympics, a major event being sponsored by the White House Office of Science and Technology.

Teenage inventors from around the country had built their own homemade robots and competed in a series of athletic competitions, testing their machines' strength, speed, and versatility. Now the winners of the four regional divisions were coming to our city to vie for the national championship. The ultimate champion would win a grand prize of $50,000, but I was more interested in the bragging rights of claiming the number-one slot. If SwiftBot came in first, I planned to donate my share of the grand prize to my favorite charity: Geeks Without Borders, a nonprofit organization committed to providing computers to schools and clinics in developing countries. Yolanda intended to do the same. "Yo and I have been tweaking his b-ball programming ever since the last meet. I think we've finally worked out most of the bugs."

"Well, good luck, bro," Sandy said. "Philly and I will definitely be there to cheer on SwiftBot."

A sleek gray tabby meowed at her feet. No doubt provoked by the smell of the raw fish, the cat sprang into Sandy's lap. "Not now, Emma," she gently scolded her pet. Reaching into her pocket, she dug out a fluffy pink sphere about the size of a golf ball and hurled it into the corridor outside the dining room. "Go chase!"

"Works every time," Sandy said with a chuckle. She had constructed the cat toy herself to occupy Emma whenever Sandy was too busy to keep throwing the ball herself. "Too bad there's not a Cat Olympics. Emma would get the gold medal in chase for sure."

"She gets enough practice," I admitted, but refrained from pointing out that, IMHO, robots were infinitely cooler than kitties, no matter how cute. "But SwiftBot would still beat her at basketball."

Sandy stuck out her tongue at me.

"I still remember building my first robot," Dad said. He smiled nostalgically. "Of course, we didn't have integrated circuits and microchips back then, just vacuum tubes and old-fashioned pneumatic cylinders, but I was awful proud of it at the time. There was quite a commotion the first time it got loose and strolled into town!"

"I'll say!" Mom confirmed, remembering. "You practically threw all of Shopton into a panic."

Sandy rolled her eyes. "Because of that old thing?" She and I had both seen the 'bot in question, which was now on display in the lobby of Swift Enterprises. It was pretty clunky-looking by modern standards. "Boy, people spooked easily back in the day."

"Things haven't changed all that much," Dad observed. His expression grew more serious. "TRB just released another statement condemning the Robo Olympics."

"So what else is new?" I said angrily. TRB, short for The Road Back, was a nutty terrorist group that was completely opposed to modern science and technology. Its members were totally convinced that science had made the world a worse place, never mind all the amazing things the human race had achieved over the ages—like wiping out smallpox, or going to the moon. Just thinking about TRB made my blood boil, and I'm certain the feeling was mutual. As one of the premier scientific think tanks in the world, Swift Enterprises was near the top of TRB's enemies list. My family and I had survived a number of run-ins with TRB over the years, none of them pleasant. "Why don't they just give it a rest for once? Why try to spoil the competition for the rest of us?"

"Fanatics don't give up easily," Dad pointed out. "They're afraid that robots are going to replace humanity—and see the Robo Olympics as 'anti-human propaganda . . .'" Concern deepened the creases in his forehead. "I just hope that there will be plenty of security at the games. Isn't Theodora VanderMeer scheduled to attend?"

I nodded. "At the final awards ceremony." Dr. VanderMeer was a Nobel Prize-winning expert in artificial intelligence and the president's chief scientific adviser to boot. "She's going to present the grand prize to the winning robot and its inventors."

"You mean you and Yo," Sandy added optimistically.

"Here's hoping," I said, crossing my fingers.

Thirsty, I reached for the pitcher of fruit punch and refilled my glass. My fingers were still sweaty from the game, however, and I accidentally hit the rim of the cup with the spout. The glass tumbled off the table, spilling bright red punch all over the floor. "Oops!" I blurted. "My bad!"

"Don't worry about it," Mom said, calmly nibbling at a morsel of rice and eel. Dad and Sandy barely gave the spill a second glance.

One of the perks of living in the house of the future was that our home could take care of accidents like this on its own. Before I could even bend over to retrieve my unbreakable plastic glass, a team of cleaning 'bots had scurried onto the scene and begun sucking up the spilled liquid. Within seconds, not a drop remained. Emma, arriving moments later, looked distinctly disappointed that there was nothing left for her to lap up. She gave the departing robots a dirty look.

Me, I was glad to see the mess disposed of so efficiently. With any luck, SwiftBot would perform just as reliably at the upcoming Olympics.

Whether TRB liked it or not.

The Games Begin

I cruised through downtown Shopton in my red hybrid. We had lucked out with the weather, getting a clear sunny morning, so I drove with the top down, letting a cool breeze rustle my hair.

The car responded like a dream, just as I had designed it to do. Next to SwiftBot, this car was my latest pride and joy. I'd spent months assembling it, and I had equipped the car with all sorts of cutting-edge features, such as a convertible nanoplastic shell, capable of changing color and configuration on demand, and "active wheels," which automatically adjusted to changing road conditions. The SW-1, also known as the Swift Speedster, was strictly one of a kind, though Sandy was already talking about designing her own version next year.

I couldn't blame her for wanting one of her own. *Sure beats riding the bus*, I thought. In a pinch the Speedster could navigate on its own, but I was having too much fun to surrender the wheel to the onboard computer. Besides, I knew the route by heart.

SwiftBot rode shotgun beside me. Ordinarily he traveled in a special trailer that Yo and I had converted into a mobile workshop/robot garage. For the first day of the Robot Olympics, though, I figured he deserved to arrive in style.

Shopton High School was straight ahead. Our school had been selected as the site for the national finals, due in part to the excellence of its science-education programs. Swift Enterprises, among others, had donated generously to the school district over the years.

I turned into the parking lot. The opening ceremonies were still hours away, but the lot was already filling up. I eased into one of the spaces reserved for the contestants.

"There you are!" a voice called out to me.

"About time!" another voice added.

My best friends, Bud Barclay and Yolanda Aponte, were waiting for me. Yo's own set of wheels, a turquoise hybrid coupe, was parked a few spaces away.

"What's the rush?" I called back to them. The Speedster's doors opened automatically, and Swift-Bot and I stepped out onto the blacktop. Behind me, the car's nanoplastic shell extruded a glossy red top as it sealed and locked itself. "We've got plenty of time to get SwiftBot checked into the competition."

"I know, dude," Bud said with a smile. (He was a skinny, African American kid with an easygoing vibe.) "We're just giving you a hard time." He fished a digital camera from his pocket and took a few steps backward. "How about a glamour shot of you and your metallic buddy there?"

"Sure thing," I answered, putting my arm around SwiftBot's shoulders. Bud wrote for the school paper, the *Shopton Gazette*, and seldom missed an opportunity for a good story or photo op. While he clicked away with his camera, I touched base with Yo. "You get that b-ball footage I zapped you?"

"Yeah, thanks," Yolanda said. She munched on an

energy bar as she spoke. Unlike Bud, she can be pretty intense. "We should take another look at SwiftBot's software. You saw through his fake out way too easily, but I think I've kluged up a fix for that. I just need to install a few new subroutines."

"Okay," I agreed readily. With anyone else, I would have been nervous about tinkering with the robot's programming at this late date, but Yo was a genuine computer wizard, even if her athletic physique hardly fit the stereotype of the nerdy computer geek. Years of martial-arts training kept her in shape. Behind her dark brown eyes was a brain that could make even the balkiest CPU jump through hoops on command. I couldn't have asked for a better partner in this competition. "Let's open him up after the inspection. I want to defragment his hard drive one last time anyway."

Yo nodded. "We probably ought to check his neural nodes while we're at it—make sure the parallel processing can cope with the latest refinements to his 'fuzzy logic' parameters."

"Enough technospeak!" Bud protested. "My eyes are glazing over already." Bud isn't much of a science guy. He prefers actual books to technical manuals, if you can believe it, and he's even been known to write out his news stories *longhand*.

Go figure.

He plucked a pencil from behind his ear and extracted a notepad from his back pocket. "So what's the deal with this 'inspection' business anyway? Aren't SwiftBot's workings top secret or something?"

"Sort of," I explained. "Way back at the beginning of the competition, before the first regional events, contestants had to submit their basic designs and blueprints to a panel of experts in order to qualify for the games. This information is supposed to be kept confidential, though, so none of us contestants can get any inside information on the strengths and weaknesses of the other robots."

"And this inspection deal?" Bud pressed.

I shrugged my shoulders. "Before the finals actually begin, the judges get a chance to check out the robots to make sure that they're still essentially the same machines that entered the competition months ago, allowing for some fine-tuning and improvements. It's a formality mostly."

"Just the same, I'll be glad when it's over," Yo said.

"I'm always afraid that we're going to get disqualified on some technicality." She glanced at her watch. "Speaking of which, it's almost time for SwiftBot's appointment. Let's get this over with."

Leaving the parking lot, we headed for the science building, where the inspections were being held. SwiftBot walked smoothly beside us. His easy gait filled me with confidence.

My dad would have been reassured by the tight security surrounding the school grounds. Even with official passes identifying us as contestants, we still had to pass through the metal detectors like everyone else. It was a hassle, but I couldn't complain. Given TRB's attitude toward the Robo Olympics, all this security was a reasonable precaution.

Only SwiftBot got to skip the metal detectors, for obvious reasons.

"Looks like you're not the only reporter covering the event," I said to Bud as we approached the building. About a dozen journalists from various papers and cable networks turned their cameras and microphones toward us. It wasn't exactly a mob scene— this was the Robot Olympics, not the Super

Bowl—but I was glad to see the competition getting so much publicity. With luck the news coverage would increase the public's interest in robotics—and maybe even inspire a new generation of young inventors.

Take that, you TRB loonies.

"Tom! Tom Swift!" a voice called from the gang of reporters. A guy wearing a tan sports jacket rushed forward and thrust a microphone in my face. "Luke McCabe. United News Network," he said, identifying himself. He had the bland good looks, and blow-dried hair, of your typical TV newsman. "What do you think your chances are?"

I stepped closer to Yo, making sure she got her fair share of attention. "We're feeling pretty confident," I said, "although it's sure to be an exciting competition. The other contestants have to know what they're doing, or they wouldn't have made it all the way to the finals."

"What about that balance problem?" McCabe pressed. "Have you got that licked yet?"

I frowned, annoyed at the reporter for asking that question right in front of SwiftBot, even though I knew he could hardly hurt the robot's feelings. Silly,

I know, but what can I say? I couldn't help feeling protective of SwiftBot.

Yo, on the other hand, knew just how to handle the question. "You'll have to wait and find out!" she said with a grin.

McCabe liked her sound byte too. "I guess so."

A loud voice intruded on the conversation. "What're you talking to those losers for? I've got your future winner right here."

A stocky, red-haired kid emerged from the science building, accompanied by a hulking, black robot. All eyes turned toward the new arrivals.

"Oh boy," Bud said sarcastically. "Look who's here."

"Be still my heart," Yo added.

Aware of the news cameras all around, I tried not to look too ticked off. Andy Foger wasn't exactly my favorite person—for good reason.

"Hey, Swift!" he bellowed. "How's that walking junk pile of yours doing? My FugBot is going to turn your wimpy windup toy into so much scrap metal!"

Andy's dad ran Foger Utility Group, Swift Enterprise's major competitor. FUG had a well-deserved reputation for playing dirty, and so did Andy. He had been a cheat and a bully for as long as I had known him, which was way too long.

"Hi, Andy," I said coolly. We had known, of course, that Andy and his FugBot were going to be here, but that didn't mean we were happy about it. "Good luck in the games."

"Save it," he grunted. "You're the one who is going to need all the luck. FugBot's going to kick your robot's butt!"

"Is that why you've kept him thousands of miles from here?" I shot back. Even though the Fogers lived in Shopton as well, our robots had yet to compete against each other. Because his parents owned a vacation home in New Mexico, Andy had been able to enter FugBot in the Southern regional events instead. I liked to think he had avoided the East Coast meets in order to skip going head-to-head with Yo and me. "Afraid of the local competition?"

"You wish!" he said. "I was in no hurry. I knew Fug-Bot could demolish your sorry excuse for a robot anytime I wanted."

"We'll see about that!" Yo said.

I took a closer look at the silent robot beside

Andy. Like SwiftBot, FugBot was basically humanoid in shape, but bulkier and a lot more intimidating. Glossy black plastic covered his outer shell, which was all sharp angles and jagged points. Painted flames and lightning bolts customized his armor. His head resembled a human skull, with camera lenses mounted in the eye sockets. *Talk about TRB's worst nightmare*, I thought. FugBot had clearly been designed to look as scary as possible.

Knowing Andy, I also suspected that his dad's scientists and technicians had helped him with the robot, which was strictly against the rules. Andy was no dummy, but if there was a way to gain an unfair advantage, he was sure to find it. Too bad I couldn't prove anything.

Bud stepped toward Andy, who glared at him suspiciously. "What do you want, Barclay?" he snarled.

"Just to be fair, I want to talk to all the contestants." Bud flipped open his notepad. "When would be a good time for me to interview you?"

"How about no time, no way?" he said with a sneer. "I've got better things to do with my time than waste my breath on some dinky school paper." He brushed past Bud, bumping him with his shoulder. "C'mon, FugBot. Let's talk to some *real* reporters."

The menacing-looking robot stomped after him into the throng of waiting journalists.

"Just as well," I commented to Bud. "You didn't want to talk to that jerk anyway."

"Tell me about it." Bud shrugged. "Hey, I gave him a chance to tell his side of the story. Can I help it if he's too much of a jerk to take me up on it?"

Yo's dark eyes shot laser beams at Andy's back. "I can't wait for SwiftBot to teach him a lesson."

"You and me both," I agreed.

A hush fell over the gymnasium as the unlit torch rose behind the dais.

Concealed motors lifted a shining metal bowl until it was several feet above the heads of the various dignitaries assembled on the makeshift stage, which had been erected at the far end of the gym. A bunch of clear fiber-optic filaments rose from the bowl. At the moment, the transparent glass strands were practically invisible.

Above and behind the torch a giant robotic face was mounted to the wall. The sharp angles of the metallic face gazed down on the stage below, looking like a cross between the Wizard of Oz and C-3PO. Glass eyes, the size of floodlights, suddenly lit up. Twin laser beams shot from the glowing eyes, converging on the base of the torch. The crimson rays energized the bundle of fiber-optic strands so that they glowed red and yellow like artificial flames. A chorus of *oob*s and *aah*s greeted the lighting of the torch.

"Ladies and gentlemen," Mayor Glenda Klyde announced from the podium. "Welcome to the first annual Robot Olympics!"

Applause erupted from the audience that packed the bleachers on both sides of the gymnasium. Not a bad turnout. At least six hundred people had shown up for the opening ceremony, and many more were presumably watching it on TV. Who knows? Maybe someday the Robo Olympics would draw the same size crowds as the real thing?

"Pretty sweet," Yo whispered to me over the applause. "That high-tech, laser-powered torch was a good idea."

I eyed the flickering red filaments. "Me, I would have gone for an ionized plasma torch, but I guess they didn't want to risk burning the gym down."

"Yeah. Imagine that," she said dryly.

We watched the proceedings from behind a pair of thick velvet curtains, at the opposite end of the gym. The curtains had been set to hide us and the other contestants from the audience until the mayor introduced us. We listened to her speech while we waited for our cue.

"The city of Shopton is proud to host this exciting event," Mayor Klyde declared. "As the home of such distinguished leaders in the field of high technology as Swift Enterprises and the Foger Utility Group, Shopton has always embraced the future of scientific progress."

Landing the Robot Olympics had been quite a coup for our city. According to rumor, Shopton had beat out such notable contenders as Silicon Valley and Seattle.

"I'd like to thank Principal Lee and the staff of the high school for letting us make use of these fine facilities," the mayor continued. Up on the dais Ms. Lee accepted a round of applause. The principal of Shopton High was an old friend of my family—and an enthusiastic supporter of quality science education.

"And now for what you've all been waiting for: our cybernetic contenders and their brilliant young inventors. Each of these teams, I remind you, came in first in their respective regional competitions, earning them the right to compete here for the grand prize.

"From the Western division, Sue Itami and . . . RollerBot!"

The curtains opened slightly and a small Asian girl stepped into the spotlight, followed by a bright yellow robot that looked more like a tank than a person. It rolled across the floor on revolving treads, each containing three wheels apiece. An extendable metal arm rose from its squat metal chassis. A pair of sonar transmitters and receivers were mounted like headlights at the front of the vehicle. Aluminum eyelashes fluttered atop the headlights, giving the robot a whimsically feminine touch.

Interesting, I thought. The rules of the Olympics didn't require that robots look like human beings, and Sue Itami had obviously gone in another direction. There were definite advantages to this sort of design, I knew. A lower center of gravity, for one. Also, since wheels were less complicated to operate than legs, Itami could devote more of her robot's onboard computer to other tasks.

"From the Southern division, Andy Foger and . . . FugBot!"

The huge black robot stomped across the floor after Andy. FugBot looked better suited to combat than peaceful athletic competition, but I knew we shouldn't underestimate Andy's robot. He had won the Southern title after all.

"From the Northern division, Persis Chadha . . . and MechaCrawler!"

Arachnophobes in the audience gasped as the spider-like contraption scuttled out from behind the curtain along with its proud inventor, a slim girl of Indian descent. MechaCrawler had eight legs, each jointed in four places. Rubber tubes running from its artificial thorax suggested that the limbs were air powered, probably by a compressor installed in the core. A metallic green paint job made the robot look like some sort of giant insect or arthropod.

Another alternative approach, I noted. Chadha's creation represented a promising trend in modern robotics: modeling robots on insects instead of people. Many legs meant that even when some of the limbs were off the ground, MechaCrawler always had enough to maintain its balance. I had considered a similar design myself, before deciding that a humanoid robot was simply cooler. Guess Persis felt differently.

"And last but not least, from the Eastern division, Tom Swift, Yolanda Aponte, . . . and SwiftBot!"

Despite Yo's worries, SwiftBot had breezed through the final inspection, qualifying for the competition. Our robot walked between us as we joined the other contestants in the spotlight. Good thing neither of us suffered from stage fright.

The theme music from *Star Wars* thundered from the loudspeakers as we and our robots paraded across the gym, giving the audience a good look. I took advantage of the opportunity to check out RollerBot and MechaCrawler. I had seen photos and news footage of the other contestants before, but this was the first time I'd viewed them in the flesh, so to speak.

Wonder how they'll perform against SwiftBot.

"Down with robots! Sports are for human athletes!" Suddenly angry shouts interrupted the parade, as five or six audience members rose to their feet and began hollering at the top of their lungs. TRB sympathizers staging a protest? They reached into their pockets and began hurling plastic nuts and bolts at us. The tiny objects rained down on the floor of the gym. I instinctively raised my hands to protect my head, even though the plastic pieces weren't much of a threat. Out of the corner of my eye, I saw FugBot do the same.

Pretty good programming. I'd give Andy that much. . . .

"Stupid zipperheads!" Yo grumbled. Nuts and bolts bounced off her dark brown hair. "Talk about closed minds!"

"Just be grateful for the metal detectors," I told her. Getting pelted with genuine steel widgets would have been a lot more uncomfortable.

"Don't glorify mechanical monsters! Boycott the Robo Obscenity!" the protestors chanted as security guards hustled them out of the gymnasium. They had a right to their opinion, naturally, but that didn't mean they could ruin the ceremony for the rest of us. "They're going to replace all of us! You could be next!"

"What's their problem anyway?" Yo watched the departing demonstrators. "Bugs in their wetware?"

"Nah," I answered. "They've just seen too many bad sci-fi movies."

Fortunately, the rest of the ceremony went off without a hitch.

Race for the Gold

"On your marks, ready, set . . ."

The first event was an obstacle course, which had been set up on the running track at the rear of the high school. Much to my relief, we had a clear blue sky for the race. A muddy course would have made the race even harder on the four robots poised at the starting line. Yo and I stood behind SwiftBot, while the other inventors "coached" their own robots.

"Go!" shouted Mr. Radnor, Shopton High's most popular science teacher, into a microphone. Young and enthusiastic, he had sandy brown hair and a neatly trimmed beard. A whistle blew loudly.

As programmed, the robots took off down the track. They ran, rolled, or scuttled, depending on

their individual modes of locomotion. In the bleachers the crowd cheered for their favorites. Glancing over at the stands, I saw my entire family urging SwiftBot on. Sandy's best friend, Phyllis Newton, added her own cheers to the clamor. Yo's family was in the bleachers, too, while Bud stood a few yards away from the starting line, snapping photos for the paper.

My eyes quickly turned back to the race itself. The course consisted of one lap around the oval-shaped track, ending right back where the robots started, but a variety of obstacles had been set up to challenge the contestants' abilities. Nothing Swift-Bot couldn't handle, of course.

Maybe.

He got off to a good start, easily keeping pace with both FugBot and RollerBot. The wheeled robot zoomed in its lane like a driverless hot rod. MechaCrawler lagged slightly behind the others but was still in the race. I knew it was way too early to predict the winner. The real contest would begin when the robots started encountering the obstructions in their path.

"Out of the way." Mr. Radnor shooed me and the

other inventors off the course and onto the neatly trimmed lawn inside the oval. He gave Yo and I an encouraging wink. "Good luck, you two."

Within moments, the racing 'bots approached the first hazard: a large puddle of clear water. I watched intently, eager to see how each robot coped with the shallow pool.

This event was not just about speed and agility. It was also a test of how quickly the robots could make decisions—and how well. Like all of the obstacles ahead, the puddle had been positioned so the racers could go either through it or around it. Taking the detour would cost a contestant time, but depending on a robot's strengths and weaknesses, that might be the safer way to go.

"Go around!" Yo hollered at SwiftBot, although it was doubtful that he could hear her over the roar of the crowd. The rules permitted voice commands, on the grounds that even human athletes were allowed coaches, but electronic jamming devices were in place to keep anyone from operating the robots by remote control. The robots had to navigate the course on their own, even if we couldn't resist shouting out advice. "Go around!"

Most of the robots slowed as they approached the water, but FugBot didn't hesitate for a second. Instantly arriving at a decision, he turned to the left and took the long way around the puddle. Better the detour than risk slipping and falling.

Probably a good call, I thought. Balancing on two legs was tricky, at least if you're a robot. SwiftBot quickly reached the same decision and turned to the right.

Yo breathed a sigh of relief.

RollerBot's sonar headlights dipped toward the puddle—perhaps scanning its depth? Then she drove right through the puddle, throwing up a spray of white water behind her. Following the wheeled robot's lead, MechaCrawler splashed through the pool after her.

This put the two nonhumanoid robots in the lead as the racers left the water behind. Thanks to his speedy reaction, FugBot was close behind them, leaving SwiftBot trailing in fourth place. "Don't worry," I reminded Yo. "This race isn't over yet."

She had a worried expression on her face. "Let's hope not."

A good runner, SwiftBot made up a little ground in

the straightaway, closing on FugBot. All four robots were still within a few yards of one another.

The second obstacle was a set of wooden stairs. Three steps led to the top of the hazard, followed by three more leading back down to the track.

Once again FugBot didn't hesitate. The ebony robot easily scaled the timber steps, passing Roller-Bot, which also climbed the steps without too much difficulty. MechaCrawler clambered up the stairs after her.

"Go for it!" I yelled at SwiftBot. We couldn't afford to fall farther behind.

"You can do it!" Yo encouraged him.

Whether he heard us or not, SwiftBot made the right choice. He took the steps more carefully than FugBot had, and he made it up and down without any stumbles. As soon as he set foot on the rubber track once more, he sprinted after the other robots. Noticeably faster than MechaCrawler, he caught up with the multi-legged robot just before the next obstacle.

A heavy sandbag hung above the course, swinging back and forth like a pendulum. The hazard was meant to test the robots' timing and reflexes. Could they make it past the swinging sandbag without getting clobbered?

We might have a chance here, I thought. SwiftBot's basketball skills should translate over to this particular challenge. If he could catch a ball on the rebound, he should be able to dodge a swinging bag of sand.

Or so I hoped.

FugBot was the first to face the pendulum. Pausing for only a second, he chose his moment, then darted beneath the pendulum while the sandbag was still swinging away from him. Yo muttered beneath her breath as FugBot made it past the trap unscathed.

"Hah!" Andy gloated. "Like that was supposed to stop him? Take a good look, losers. That's what a *real* robot looks like!"

"He's pretty impressive," I conceded grudgingly.

"Just wait," Andy warned. "You haven't seen anything yet!"

RollerBot took a few moments to analyze the sandbag's trajectory, then accelerated beneath the pendulum in a hurry. For a second it looked like the robot's timing was slightly off. The sandbag barely missed the 'bot's rear bumper as it swung back toward RollerBot.

"Good girl!" Sue Itami cheered her creation. "You show 'em!"

SwiftBot was still timing the arc of the pendulum when MechaCrawler went for it. Eight shining metal legs moved in unison as the robotic spider chased after the first two racers. I winced at the sight, afraid that SwiftBot was going to get left in the dust again.

But MechaCrawler had been too impatient. The sandbag came swinging back toward the spider-bot before it made through the trap, and slammed into MechaCrawler like a battering ram, knocking the robot all the way off the track. The crowd gasped out loud.

"Oh, no!" Persis Chadha exclaimed. I couldn't help feeling sorry for her.

"Tough break," I offered in sympathy.

"Thanks," she said, looking mortified by her robot's mistake.

Andy hooted in delight. "Did you see that? Wham! What a wipeout!"

Back on the track, SwiftBot didn't wait to see if

MechaCrawler would recover from the collision. A motor atop the pendulum had kept the sandbag swinging, but SwiftBot chose his moment and dashed past the hazard without being tagged.

"Yes!" I blurted. "That's the way! Keep going!"

Now we just had to catch up with FugBot and RollerBot. Andy's robot had a substantial lead, though. We could only hope that one of the remaining obstacles would trip him up.

Meanwhile, MechaCrawler proved to be of sturdy construction. Despite its bruising encounter with the sandbag, it scrambled back onto the track and came at the pendulum once more. This time the spider-bot managed to evade the sandbag, but found itself way behind the other racers. Could it still make up the ground it had lost?

Probably not, I decided. Unless the rest of us all screwed up on the last two hazards.

The next challenge was a row of ordinary track hurdles, like human athletes jump over. The hardened plastic gates were lined up side by side and set thirty inches above the track. Not much of a challenge for a flesh-and-blood track star but quite a leap for a robot. We had tested SwiftBot on similar hurdles with mixed results. *Sometimes* he would make it over the hurdle, but only sometimes.

Had Andy run into the same problem? I prayed the hurdle would slow FugBot down, maybe even force him to take a detour around it, but no such luck. Yo groaned beside me as the glossy black robot cleared the hurdle in front of him with ease. Landing nimbly on the track, he kept on running without even breaking his stride.

My heart sank. Was there anything Andy's robot couldn't do?

RollerBot faced the hurdle next, but she wasn't exactly built for jumping. Turning right, she chose to take the long way around the row of hurdles.

"Darn it," Sue Itami sighed. "I *knew* this was going to be a problem. . . ."

All right! RollerBot's difficulty with the hurdles gave SwiftBot a chance to pull into second place—if he could clear the hurdle like FugBot had.

Holding our breaths, Yo and I watched as our robot neared the barrier. Seconds before colliding with the hurdle, he launched himself off the ground. His right leg was extended before him while his left leg whipped up behind him. *Good form*, I thought. In order to prepare SwiftBot for this event, Yo and I had boned up on the biomechanics of jumping hurdles.

He *almost* made it, but . . . no! His left heel clipped the top of the gate, knocking the entire hurdle over. SwiftBot stumbled forward.

"Yikes!" Yo yelped. She threw her hands in front of her face, peeking out through her fingers. "I'm afraid to look!"

I knew how she felt. For a second I was scared that he was going to fall flat on his metal face. SwiftBot managed a partial recovery, however, landing on one knee instead. He quickly sprang back onto his feet and kept on running.

"Good save!" I shouted. "Don't give up!"

But SwiftBot's stumble had cost him his chance to get ahead of RollerBot, who completed her detour around the hurdles and came zooming back down the track beside him. As the four robots closed in on the final obstacle, FugBot was way in the lead with Swift-Bot and RollerBot fighting it out for second place. MechaCrawler, who had gone around the hurdles as well, was a distant fourth.

The last of the challenges was another puddle, but

this time we weren't talking plain old ordinary water. A slippery pool of oil awaited the robots as they rounded the curve, heading into the final stretch of the race. Iridescent rainbows gleamed on the greasy surface of the pool.

As before, FugBot made his decision in an instant. Carefully avoiding the oil slick, he turned and ran around the edges of the puddle. *So much for first place*, I thought glumly. FugBot had the race all locked up.

"This is too easy!" Andy gloated. I didn't need to look at him to imagine the smug look on his face. "Those other robots are jokes!"

Yo glowered at Andy, looking like she wanted to practice her martial-arts moves on his skull. "Thanks for not bragging about it!"

We still had a chance at second place, though. SwiftBot and RollerBot were neck and neck (even though, technically, RollerBot didn't have a neck). They reached the outer edge of the oil slick at about the same time.

"Around!" Yo shouted. She was practically jumping up and down in her excitement. "Go around that mess!"

SwiftBot wisely took her advice.

RollerBot did not.

The wheeled robot tried to plow straight through the oil, just like she had the water, but the treacherous grease was more slippery than she had anticipated. Losing traction, she spun around wildly, out of control. Sue Itami moaned and buried her face in her hands.

I sympathized, but I was glad to see RollerBot run into trouble.

Bypassing the slick entirely, SwiftBot charged ahead of the wheeled robot and across the finish line—nearly a minute after FugBot.

Not quite the outcome I wanted.

A few minutes later, Mr. Radnor announced the results of the race:

"Fourth place . . . MechaCrawler.

"Third place . . . RollerBot

"Second place . . . SwiftBot

"And, in first place, FugBot!"

Was it just my imagination or was the crowd's applause somewhat less enthusiastic? Andy didn't have a whole lot of friends in Shopton aside from the creeps who hung out with him because he had plenty of money to spend. The Fogers were more feared than admired around here. I spotted Andy's dad, Randall Foger, in the stands, surrounded by bodyguards and assistants. He was a bald, stocky man with a ruddy complexion. A company photographer snapped numerous shots of Andy and his victorious robot.

"This sucks," Yo said. "What a lousy way to start the games."

"There are still two more events," I reminded her. Weight lifting and basketball. "Andy hasn't beaten us yet."

"That's right!" she agreed. Her dark eyes gleamed defiantly. "SwiftBot has not yet begun to fight!"

Still, it was only good sportsmanship to congratulate Andy on his victory. We walked across the field to where he was posing with FugBot for the news photographers. My eyes scanned the robot's forbidding black armor. As much as I hated to admit it, FugBot had been absolutely astounding in the obstacle course.

"Congratulations, Andy." I offered him my hand. "FugBot did great."

"He deserved to win," Yo conceded. "I wish I knew how you programmed him to figure out all those obstacles so fast."

"Get used to it, losers!" Andy said.

5

Field Trip to the Future

The gleaming skyscraper rose like a spire on the outskirts of town. Fifteen stories high, the headquarters of Swift Enterprises was an imposing glass-and-steel edifice incorporating loads of environmentally friendly innovations. A vertical-axis wind turbine spun atop the spire, generating much of the building's electricity. Rainwater collectors piped any precipitation into the plumbing and cooling systems. Shredded paper and food scraps made their way into a massive composting vat, where the trash was eventually converted into fuel to power another electrical generator. An automated mower neatly trimmed the lawn in front of the building.

"Here we are," I said as the limousine pulled into the gated parking lot. "The heart—or maybe the brain—of Swift Enterprises."

"Cool!" Sue Itami enthused. Along with Yo and Bud, all of the competing inventors were in the limo with me. "Thanks for arranging this tour."

"Yes, this is very nice of you," Persis Chadha added.

"No problem," I said. "Since we're in my backyard, so to speak, it's only fair that I show you around."

A day off had been scheduled between events to give us time to perform any needed repairs or maintenance on our robots. As a friendly gesture I had volunteered to give the visiting inventors a tour of SE headquarters. If nothing else, I figured, it would give us all a chance to get to know one another a little better.

I was already getting a sense of the other contestants' personalities.

Sue, the creator of RollerBot, was funny and outgoing. Fluorescent purple dye streaked her hair. Anime characters were printed on her T-shirt. She and Yo had hit it off immediately. "Have you read *FullMetal Alchemist?*" she asked Yo. "It's, like, the best manga ever!"

"Even better than *Rurouni Kenshin*?" Yo asked.

"Way better," Sue insisted. "I'll loan you my copy. You have *got* to read it!"

Persis was more on the shy side. A thin girl with straight black hair, she appeared uncomfortable making eye contact. Bud was trying to interview her for the school paper, but he was having trouble getting her to open up. "C'mon," he urged her. "Tell me more about yourself. How'd you first get interested in robots?"

She shrugged and stared at her feet. "There's not much to tell. I guess I just have a knack for building things." Peering out the window, she made an obvious attempt to change the subject. "That's quite a building. Very modern looking."

"Hah!" Andy snorted. "You think that's something, you should see the FUG building on the other side of town. I'd invite you over, but no can do. My dad's projects are too important and hush-hush to let just anybody into the building." He nodded at me. "I'm sure Swift here would just love to get a peek at our secrets."

"Yeah, right," I replied. Frankly, I already knew

Andy better than I would have liked, but it would have been rude not to invite him along with the other contestants. "If any company is into industrial espionage, it's FUG, not SE."

"Watch it, Swift!" Andy bristled. "That's slander, you know. I'll sic my dad's lawyers on you."

"Okay, *alleged* industrial espionage," I corrected myself. "Anyway, now's not the time to argue about this. Let's just enjoy our day off."

The limo came to a stop in front of the building, and we all piled out of the car. The security guards at the entrance were expecting us, so we walked right in. The spacious lobby was decorated with glass display cases containing many of my dad's early inventions, including a photo telephone, a magnetic silencer, a g-force inverter, and an electron retroscope. His famous runaway robot stood proudly in one corner. Compared to SwiftBot, it looked like an oversize kid's toy. Scale models of various experimental ships and aircraft hung from the ceiling. Glancing upward, I recognized my dad's diving seacopter, ultrasonic cycloplane, and triphibian atomicar, among many other futuristic vehicles.

"What a bunch of junk," Andy muttered.

Nobody else seemed to share his opinion. "Hey, look at that!" Sue exclaimed. She ran across the lobby to get a better look at my dad's old robot. "That is seriously retro—in a cool way, that is."

I noticed that Persis was still trying to blend into the background. "MechaCrawler looks great," I said, walking toward her. "What inspired you to try an insect-based design?"

"It just seemed a logical way to go," she said meekly. "On a practical level, robotics is still in its infancy, so why not start out by imitating a simple life form instead of something more complex?" Her voice perked up as she warmed to the subject. "Insects have been walking around for more than four hundred million years, so they must be doing something right."

I laughed at her remark. "Good point!"

Unfortunately, Andy heard us talking. "Your stupid spider didn't do so great yesterday, did it?" He sneered at Persis, who flinched at his harsh words. "The competition must have been pretty weak in your division if that fourth-place wonder was the best they could come up with."

"That's enough," I said firmly, stepping between

61

him and Persis. I wasn't about to let Andy bully someone right in front of me. "Try to remember that you're here as a guest, Andy. Don't make me have you escorted from the premises."

"Whatever," he said, trudging away. "Can I help it if you losers don't have a sense of humor?"

I continued the tour. "Follow me, everybody."

My dad was tied up in meetings all day, so I figured we'd skip the executive offices upstairs. Instead we took an elevator down to the first of several subbasements located beneath the building. This was where the *really* interesting stuff went on.

"Next stop: Laboratory A-33," I announced.

"Are all Swift products manufactured underground?" Sue asked as the elevator descended. "How very Bruce Wayne of you."

"Only the prototypes," I explained. "SE is a think tank, not a factory. We develop the basic ideas and patents here, but any mass production occurs elsewhere. We have plants and research centers all over the world."

"So does FUG," Andy insisted. "Except ours are bigger and better."

Yo rolled her eyes. "Give it a rest, Foger."

I smiled but kept my mouth shut. Maybe the best way to handle Andy's big mouth was just to ignore it.

The elevator doors slid open to reveal an elderly man wearing a rumpled white lab coat. "Welcome!" he said, peering at us through a pair of old-fashioned bifocals. A receding hairline exposed his smooth brown scalp. His lab coat was stained by unknown chemicals and acid burns. "Are you ready to get a sneak preview of the future?"

Dr. Victor Rashid is the head scientist and lab director at SE. He holds advanced degrees in physics, engineering, chemistry, aeronautics, and just about any other scientific discipline you might think of. He was my father's favorite teacher in college, and he has been in charge of the labs here for as long as I can remember. Although physically frail, he remains mentally sharper than most people.

"You bet!" I introduced him to the other inventors. "Thanks for taking the time to show us around."

"It's my pleasure," he insisted. "Where would the future be without young people to live in it?" He guided us toward a sliding glass door at the end of the hall. "Naturally, certain laboratories are off-limits to visitors, no matter how talented, but we're working on a few projects in here that may intrigue you."

Through the doorway we found ourselves in a large workshop populated by maybe a half dozen SE technicians and researchers. Computer banks and work counters lined the walls. The buzz of excited conversations rose above the classic rock playing softly in the background. Soundproof tiles kept the noise from escaping into the hall. Fire extinguishers, and a couple of scorch marks, hinted at the occasional experimental mishap.

Prototypes of new inventions, in various stages of completion, were scattered throughout the work area. In one corner an inkjet the size of a refrigerator was sliding along an overhead carriage, "printing" walls of fast-setting concrete. Not far away a team of workers was busy assembling a new deep-sea submersible. A couple of giddy techs hurled handfuls of mud and paint at another worker who was wearing a pristine white dress. The gloppy messes slid right off the stain-resistant fabric, leaving the dress looking as good as new.

"Wow!" Sue exclaimed. She and the other visitors gazed around wide-eyed, uncertain where to look first. Even Andy looked impressed, despite himself. "I could use some clothes like that," Sue added. "Especially during my next paintball tournament."

"Take a look at this," Dr. Rashid suggested. He led us toward one corner, where a boxlike device rested atop a stainless-steel counter. It looked a lot like a microwave oven, complete with a clear plastic window looking in on the hollow interior. "This unit is part of our effort to perfect a working claytronic fabricator."

"A what?" Bud asked.

"Sort of a 3-D fax machine," the old scientist explained. "The idea is to scan an object at one location, then generate a three-dimensional facsimile of that object at the other end of a transmission." He gestured toward a similar unit several yards away. "Observe."

Removing his wristwatch, he placed it inside the unit, then tapped out a command on the attached keypad. Through the clear plastic window, we watched as ruby-colored laser beams scanned the watch from every direction. I half expected the watch to vanish, but instead it remained where it was. Actual teleportation was still down the road, I guess.

Still, this seemed like a step in the right direction.

While the watch was being scanned, Dr. Rashid herded us over to the second unit. Peering inside the device, we saw a shapeless blob of purple clay sitting within. At least it started out shapeless. Before our eyes, the clay began shifting and moving, as though being sculpted by invisible hands. "How?" Yo asked in amazement.

"Programmable matter," Dr. Rashid said. "Each molecule of the clay is actually a micron-sized mobile computer in communication with the other molecules. Working together, they can assemble themselves into a wide variety of configurations."

Within minutes a clay duplicate of the watch had formed inside the fabricator. He reached in and extracted the copy. "Careful," he said, handing it over to me. "It's still a bit fragile."

The clay watch was also noticeably slimy to the touch. We passed it among ourselves.

"Does it actually work?" Persis asked in a hushed tone. She sounded almost frightened at the prospect. "Like a real watch?"

"Sadly, no," Dr. Rashid admitted. "At the moment, we can only duplicate the shape and appearance of the transmitted objects, not their fundamental properties."

"Even still, that's pretty amazing." I could already foresee all sorts of practical applications. "My mom could send copies of her sculptures across the country just by pressing a few buttons. Or a doctor could instantly transmit a 3-D model of a patient's heart or brain to a specialist on the other side of the world."

"Exactly!" Dr. Rashid said. "In theory one could also use this technology to create smaller or larger versions of an object, just as easily as hitting enlarge or reduce on a copy machine." He reclaimed the real watch from the transmitter. "Of course, we've still got a few bugs to work out first."

"No kidding!" Andy said scornfully. He poked the duplicate with his finger and it crumbled into pieces. "Oops."

"See here, young man!" Dr. Rashid protested. He knew exactly who Andy was, of course. "I didn't tolerate that sort of attitude from your father when he was my student, and I'm not going to accept it from the next generation, either. Mind your manners!"

Andy was caught off guard by the old man's stern tone. "Yessir!" he said, swallowing hard. He took an involuntary step backward and mumbled an apology. "Sorry about that."

I tried not to grin too obviously.

Q.U.I.P. interrupted the awkward moment. "Hey!" the AI spoke from my wristwatch. "Don't forget that banquet you've got coming up in a few hours. Better wrap things up."

"Right," I said, grateful for the reminder. The Robo Olympics Committee had scheduled a dinner with the contestants this evening. Dr. VanderMeer, the president's science adviser, hadn't arrived in Shopton yet, but many other prominent scientists and educators were going to be at the banquet. I had to give everybody a chance to get ready for the dinner.

"Well, that's all the time we have," I announced. "Thanks again for the demonstration, Dr. Rashid."

We took the elevator back to the lobby and headed toward the front exit. Before we could step outside, however, a gruff voice called out to us. "Hold on there! Stay right where you are!"

I turned around to see Harlan Ames, SE's head of security, striding toward us, along with a couple of uniformed security guards. A former FBI agent, Ames had lost his right leg in a terrorist bombing a few years back, but you'd never know it from the brisk way he marched across the lobby. My dad had fitted him with a custom-made prosthetic leg even before the injured agent had come to work for him.

"What's the problem?" I asked. Ames took his job very seriously. I knew he wouldn't have detained us without a good reason.

"We have a disturbance outside," Ames said. He had short gray hair and a craggy face that seldom smiled. "Probably nothing serious, but my team and I will escort you to your car."

As we exited the building, I saw what Ames was worried about. A large mob of protestors had gathered in front of the building, just outside the front gates. They waved signs and banners bearing anti-robot slogans. When they saw us emerge from the skyscraper, they started chanting in unison.

"Make friends, not monsters! Stay away from the Frankenstein factory!"

Somehow TRB had found out about our tour and seen an opportunity to generate some publicity for their cause. A handful of reporters, including Luke McCabe from UNN, had shown up to cover the demonstration. Vans from most of the local TV stations were parked outside the gate. A news copter hovered overhead. *Terrific*, I thought.

Even Bud snapped a couple of pictures of the protest. He gave me an apologetic look. "Sorry, Tom."

"It's okay," I told him. News was news. I didn't expect him to ignore a genuine news event just to spare my feelings. Besides, Bud had written loads of positive stories about my inventions over the years. "You're just doing your job."

Ames and his people shepherded us into the waiting limo, then kept the protestors clear of the drive as our car left Swift Enterprises by way of the front gate. From inside the limo, we could see the angry mob shout and wave their signs at us.

"What a bunch of losers!" Andy growled. For once, I agreed with him. At least FUG wasn't anti-science like TRB.

"Duh. Don't they know they can't turn back the clock?" Sue added. "Newsflash: The robot genie is out of the bottle."

"They're insane!" Persis said vehemently. "They don't know what they're talking about!"

Persis's intensity surprised me. And I thought *I* didn't like TRB and its supporters! I couldn't help wondering why the otherwise quiet girl was so emotional on this issue.

If I didn't know better, I would have thought she was protesting too much.

Several hours later, after the dinner, I was driving Bud and Yo home in my Speedster when an idea struck me. "Hey, Yo. Suppose we temporarily replace some of the shock absorbers in SwiftBot's feet with spent-uranium plugs? That would lower his center of gravity and make his footing more solid."

Tomorrow was the weight lifting contest, and I was all about finding ways to improve the robot's stability.

Yo's eyes lit up. "That could work! I'll have to adjust his ambulatory subroutines, but how hard can that be?"

"Don't ask me," Bud joked. "I have no idea what you guys are talking about."

I glanced at Bud. "Mind if we make a detour?" The weight lifting event was scheduled for eleven in the morning, so Yo and I had to get to work right away if we wanted to get SwiftBot upgraded in time for the event.

"Go ahead," he said agreeably. "I wouldn't want to stand between SwiftBot and a gold medal. Here's hoping he performs like Atlas at tomorrow's competition."

"Who?" I asked.

"Atlas . . . from Greek mythology? The Titan who supported the weight of the earth on his shoulders?" He rolled his eyes at my blank expression. "Never mind," he said with a smile. "I should have known better than to wax mythological in this crowd."

Bud liked to tease me, in a friendly way, about just how little I knew about history and literature and all that nonscience stuff. What can I say? I'm an inventor, not a book reviewer. If it doesn't have a circuit diagram in it, I probably haven't read it.

The banquet had run late, so it was nearly midnight when we arrived at Shopton High, where the robots were residing for the duration of the games. A fenced-off section of the parking lot held the robots' individual trailers. A security guard had been posted to protect the robots from prying eyes or attempts at sabotage.

We parked outside the chain-link fence and walked up to the gate. The guard examined our passes, then let us through. After our run-in with those anti-robot nuts outside my dad's building, I definitely appreciated all the precautions that had been taken to keep our robots safe. Even though all the demonstrations had been peaceful so far, I knew that TRB would like nothing better than to smash SwiftBot and his fellow 'bots to pieces.

If not worse.

It was a cool summer evening. Murky shadows were draped over the silent lot, which was lit only by the occasional streetlight. My laser pointer doubled as a flashlight, helping us make our way toward SwiftBot's trailer, which was located near the rear of the lot. An eerie stillness hung over the scene. Chances were, the rest of the inventors were all getting a good night's sleep, resting up for tomorrow's event. Apparently, no one else was doing any last-minute tinkering tonight. We seemed to have the whole place to ourselves.

Or did we?

The hiss of a soda can being popped open startled me. I swung the flashlight beam toward the sound.

The light revealed a stranger standing outside one of the other trailers. He was older than we were, in his late twenties maybe, with curly red hair and a thick mustache. Gym attire clothed his athletic build. His face looked vaguely familiar, but I couldn't place it.

Who in the world?

"What the—!" the man blurted. He blinked against the glare of the flashlight. His startled expression made it clear that he was just as surprised as we were. The can slipped from his fingers and crashed onto the pavement.

Bud quickly snapped a photo of the stranger.

"Hey!" I called out. "What are you doing here?"

Instead of answering, the man swore under his breath and held a hand up in front of his face. We hurried toward him, but the man ducked inside the trailer and slammed the door shut before we got there.

"Hello?" Yo knocked on the door of the trailer, but no one answered. "C'mon, we know you're in there!"

But the man inside didn't respond.

After a few more knocks, Yo gave up and stepped back from the door. She gave Bud and me a puzzled look. "Too weird," she commented. "What was that all about?"

"I don't know," I said, "but take a look at this."

The beam of my flashlight exposed an ugly corporate logo on the side of the trailer. Block letters spelled out F-U-G on top of a cartoon drawing of Earth.

Talk about delusions of grandeur.

"This is FugBot's trailer," Yo realized. "But who was that dude?"

"Maybe some guy Andy hired to babysit FugBot?" Bud suggested. "That's not against the rules, is it?"

"No," I admitted. "But why didn't he want us to see him?" He obviously hadn't expected anyone else to be outside the trailers at this hour. "He looked familiar, like I've seen him before somewhere."

"I thought so too," Bud said, checking the display on his digital camera. Peering over his shoulder, I saw that Bud had gotten a good shot of the guy before he hid his face from the camera. He showed it to Yo, who shook her head. "Well, maybe it will come to me later," Bud said.

"Count on it," I said. A born reporter, Bud was good at digging up obscure bits of data, even if he barely knew his way around a hard drive.

"Should we report this to the guard out front?" Yo asked.

"Probably," I said. "This may all be perfectly legit, like Bud says, but it couldn't hurt to say something to the guard. Just in case there's something fishy going on." A glance at my wristwatch revealed that it was already five after twelve. "On the other hand, we've still got a robot to upgrade before morning."

"I'll go talk to the guard," Bud volunteered. "You two head to your trailer. I'll meet you there."

"Sounds like a plan," I agreed. "Thanks."

"You're a lifesaver!" Yo added.

Bud trotted back toward the gate, while Yo and I left Andy's trailer behind and proceeded toward our own mobile workshop. My brain started to switch gears, focusing on the job ahead. How else could we increase his lifting capacity? Maybe by reinforcing his knee joints?

My flashlight beam found the trailer, and a flicker of movement caught my attention. A shape up on the roof hastily ducked out of sight.

Yo saw it too. "Tom!" she exclaimed. "There's somebody on the roof!"

What in the world? For a supposedly secure site, the trailers' lot was turning out to be surprisingly crowded tonight. Was this the same stranger we had just spotted outside FugBot's trailer? But there was no way that guy could have gotten here before us. This was someone else.

But who?

I rushed angrily toward the trailer, with Yo right behind me. "Hey, get down from there!" I shouted. "What do you think you're doing?"

A muffled curse came from atop the trailer. I heard the intruder scrambling on the roof, followed by the sound of someone landing heavily on the pavement on the other side. Footsteps pounded on the asphalt as the stranger made a break for it.

"He's getting away!" I shouted. Running around the side of the trailer, I spotted the mysterious figure racing for the nearby fence. Forget that. No way was I going to let this guy escape before I found out what he was up to. "Stop right there!" I hollered after him. "You'd better have a pretty good explanation for all this!"

The stranger glanced back over his shoulder at me. A black ski mask concealed his features. A dark track suit offered no clue as to his identity. I got the impression that he was an adult, but I couldn't be sure.

The chain-link fence was only about forty feet ahead of the stranger. I was gaining on him, though, and figured I could grab him before he made it over the fence. I'd tackle him if I had to. "Give it up!" I yelled. "You're not going anywhere!"

The stranger reached into the pocket of his track suit and pulled out a handful of glass capsules. Twisting at the waist, he hurled them back toward me. I ducked instinctively, but the capsules hit the pavement in front of me instead. Glass shattered noisily, and a greasy fluid spread over the blacktop directly in my path. I tried to skid to a halt, but momentum carried me forward onto the slippery mess. Suddenly, I knew what RollerBot had felt like when she hit that oil slick yesterday.

My feet slid out from beneath me, and I toppled backward, landing hard on my butt. "Ouch!" I tried to scramble back onto my feet, but that was easier said than done. Struggling to get free of the slick, I watched helplessly as the stranger in the ski mask scaled the fence and dropped onto the ground outside the lot. He disappeared into the night, leaving plenty of unanswered questions behind.

Who was that guy anyway? And what was he doing on top of our trailer?

A scarier question hit me. Was SwiftBot all right? Stumbling forward on my knees, I made it onto dry pavement again and jumped to my feet. My pants were soaked with oil, but, thankfully, I had managed to avoid getting cut on any glass slivers. Wiping my greasy hands on my shirt, I cast a final glance at the darkness outside the fence before hurrying back to our trailer.

"Yo?" At first, I didn't see my partner anywhere.

"Up here!" she called out. I looked up to see Yo crouching on the roof of the trailer, right where the prowler had been. "Look what I found!"

She lobbed a tiny metallic object off the roof and into my hands. Beneath the soft white glow of the nearest streetlight, I could see I was holding a magnetic steel wafer about the size of a matchbook. A miniature antenna protruded from the object.

"Some sort of listening device?" I guessed.

Yo nimbly dropped onto the pavement. "That's

what I figure," she agreed. "That crook was bugging our trailer!" She tapped the wall of the trailer with her knuckles. "SwiftBot's fine, by the way. I checked on him while you were chasing after the creep. What happened there anyway?"

I explained how the stranger had gotten away from me. Yo eyed my oil-stained clothes. "No offense, buddy," she said, wrinkling her nose, "but you smell like a gas station."

"Tell me about it," I said. "Dr. Rashid can't perfect that spill-proof fabric fast enough." The gloppy condition of my clothes was the least of my worries, though. I stared at the ominous listening device in my palm.

Who had attempted to bug our trailer?
And why?

6

Heavy Lifting

"Fess up, Andy! This is another one of your dirty tricks, isn't it?"

The next morning the other contestants and I were all hanging out in the school parking lot. The weight lifting competition had been postponed until the afternoon while the authorities investigated last night's bugging incident. The slim metallic wafer had indeed turned out to be a covert listening device, which meant that someone had definitely been trying to spy on what happened in SwiftBot's trailer.

The more I thought about it, the more I felt certain that Andy Foger was that "someone." From what

I had seen of the guy in the ski mask, he hadn't looked much like Andy, but that didn't mean Andy hadn't hired someone else to do his dirty work. This was exactly the kind of slimy stunt I expected from him.

"You're nuts, Swift!" Andy bellowed. "I didn't have anything to do with this. You're just trying to frame me—like you always do." He sneered and stuck his face in my space. "How do I know you didn't plant that bug yourself?"

"Now who's talking crazy?" Yo argued, backing me up. "And what was with that guy we saw lurking outside your trailer last night? He sure acted like he was up to no good!"

Andy copped an attitude. "I already explained that to the committee. That was just some dude I hired to keep an eye on FugBot when I'm not around." He smirked smugly. "Sounds like I had the right idea, too, considering all the suspicious characters running around this lot last night."

He looked pointedly at me.

"Oh yeah?" Yo said. She wasn't buying it. "So how come that guy was acting so guilty last night? He couldn't get out of sight fast enough!"

Andy shrugged. "What can I say? You must have spooked him, Aponte." He snorted at the thought. "'Besides, why are you giving *me* a hard time?" He pointed at Sue and Persis. "Why aren't you giving those two the third degree? They're from out of town. We don't know a darn thing about them."

"And I already trust them more than you!" Yo shot back.

With good reason, I thought. Andy's track record argued against him. Still, he had a point. There were *four* robots in these games, and a grand prize of $50,000 was at stake. We all had a motive for spying on the others.

"Hey, chill out, everybody!" Sue protested. "Let's not get all paranoid, at least until we know what's really going down."

"Yes," Persis said. She wrung her hands together. "Can't we just get along?"

"Okay," I said. Maybe it had been a mistake to accuse Andy without any evidence, even though I still had my suspicions. "I'll let it drop . . . for now."

"Gee, that's big of you, Swift," Andy said sarcastically. "Remind me to send you a gift basket."

I'd rather have an e-mail full of spam, I thought, but bit my tongue. Sue was right. There was no point in prolonging this discussion until we knew more. Plus, we had a competition coming up, assuming that the weight lifting event wasn't postponed again. At least Yo and I had managed to upgrade SwiftBot last night, after everything quieted down.

A yawn escaped my lips. It had been a long night.

"Tom! Yo!" I turned to see Bud running toward us. He had been covering the investigation for the *Gazette.* "I've got news!"

He slowed to a stop, and we all crowded around him. Everyone, including Andy, seemed anxious to hear what he had to say.

"What is it?" I asked.

"Spill, pal!" Yo urged him.

Bud paused to catch his breath. "First off, there's no word on who your mystery man was. The cops checked out your whole trailer but didn't find any incriminating fingerprints on the roof. Or anywhere else."

That sucked. I wondered if I could whip up a portable DNA scanner before lunch.

Probably not. That would be pushing it, even for me.

"Didn't they find anything?" Yo asked.

"Wait," Bud said. "Here's the weird part. They found more bugs—on all four of the trailers!"

"Huh?"

"What?"

"No kidding?"

"Really?"

"No!"

I couldn't believe my ears. All four trailers had been bugged? Even Andy's?

"*Trés* bizarro!" Yo blurted. "Who would do something like that?"

"TRB?" I guessed. I remembered the demonstration outside my dad's building yesterday and all the news cameras that had been on hand to cover the story. "An overzealous reporter?" Although I hated to admit it, this latest development seemed to clear Andy's name—unless he bugged himself just to divert suspicion. *Always a possibility*, I reminded myself. Andy was sneaky, not stupid. "Maybe a big-time gambler betting on the games?"

"This doesn't sound like TRB," Yo said. "Bombs are more their style."

"Bombs?" Persis repeated nervously.

"Sure," Sue informed her. "Remember that explosion at the computer chess finals a few years back? That was TRB." She made a face, like she was smelling hydrogen sulfide. "What a bunch of future phobes!"

Bud flipped through his notepad. "I don't get it. What's the point in bugging the trailers now? The robots are already built, aren't they?"

"True," I admitted. "But a spy might still be able to figure out what an individual robot's weaknesses are by listening in while it's being worked on. For example, you might discover that an opposing robot has a balance problem or a limited range of vision, and adjust your own robot's programming to take advantage of that flaw."

Good thing we had caught that guy last night. Before Yo and I got busy upgrading SwiftBot.

"Right. I get it now," Bud said. "It's all about getting the inside scoop on the competition."

"Exactly," Yo said. "I just wish we knew who was behind it!"

Despite the bugging scandal, the weight lifting competition started promptly at two. An impressive crowd filled the bleachers inside the gym, and there were at least twice as many camera crews as there were before the incident. I guess what they said was true: All publicity is good publicity.

Me, I could have done without this particular news angle.

All four robots were lined up on the floor of the gym, each facing a cable-and-pulley system attached to a number of weighted iron plates. Because the robots came in such varied sizes and shapes, the committee had decided that this sort of pull-down setup provided the fairest test of strength. After all, without humanoid bodies, MechaCrawler and RollerBot could hardly hoist barbells the way a flesh-and-blood weight lifter would.

Instead, the competing robots would each pull on a reinforced steel cable in their attempts to raise ever-increasing weights. The winner would be the 'bot that could lift the heaviest load.

Yo and I stood on an exercise mat alongside Swift-Bot. "Good luck, Swifty," she said, giving the robot an affectionate pat on the back. "We're counting on you."

I'll say, I thought. This was our big chance to pull

out of second place—and ahead of FugBot. "We should have a good shot at winning this."

"You'd think," Yo agreed.

We had modeled SwiftBot's muscles after the human variety, using something called "muscle wire." These were threads of titanium-nickel alloy that contracted whenever an electric current passed through them, mimicking the action of genuine human muscles. When the current stopped, the wire returned to its original length, just like a muscle relaxing. Muscle wire was more realistic than motors or inflatable balloons, like some robots used, and stronger, too. One thread could lift thousands of times its own weight.

But would that be enough to beat the other robots? We were about to find out.

The competition would start at one hundred pounds. Robo Olympics officials loaded up each cable machine with a single hundred-pound plate. "Take your positions!" Mr. Radnor announced into his microphone. In the bleachers, the crowd leaned forward in anticipation.

"Begin lifting routine," I instructed SwiftBot. He took hold of a metal handlebar with both hands. To lift the weight, he would have to walk backward while pulling on the cable.

I glanced around at the other robots to see what they were doing. To my left MechaCrawler had grabbed onto its handlebar with its two front legs, leaving it with six more to walk on. To my immediate right, RollerBot had seized her own grip with her single, cranelike arm. Two mats down, FugBot was using both hands like SwiftBot. All the robots looked primed to begin.

"On your mark," Mr. Radnor said. He walked back and forth behind the weights. "Ready, set . . . lift!"

"Go!" I told SwiftBot.

It wasn't a race. This contest was about strength, not speed. Every robot who managed to lift the hundred pounds in the allotted ninety seconds would go on to the next heat. Yo and I cheered SwiftBot on as he backed away from the cable machine, lifting the heavy steel plate from the floor until it was the required five feet above the mat. A ref raised his hand, signaling that SwiftBot had completed the lift successfully.

"That's it!" I said. "You did it!"

"Good job!" Yo chimed in.

To be honest, we weren't too surprised that our robot had gotten through the first round okay. We knew SwiftBot could lift a mere hundred pounds. The real challenge would come later, when the weights got heavier.

Looking around, I saw that all four robots had survived the first heat without too much difficulty. As SwiftBot slowly lowered the hundred-pound plate back onto its base, I took a moment to rate the competition.

Was anybody else using muscle wire?

It didn't look like it. MechaCrawler's multiple limbs were all powered by pneumatic cylinders. Not a very sophisticated design, IMHO, but sturdy and reliable. I remembered what Persis had said about how insect bodies had worked fine for more than four hundred million years. Who knows, maybe she was on to something? Everyone knew that ants and spiders could lift many times their own weight.

RollerBot might be a real threat too. After all, the wheeled robot looked like a piece of heavy construction equipment. With her tanklike treads and motorized arm, it wasn't hard to imagine Sue's robot competing in an old-fashioned tractor pull . . . and winning.

And then there was FugBot. Who knew what kind of mechanics were hidden inside that robot's plastic armor. Air muscles? Hydraulics? Electric motors? FugBot had proved the fastest in the obstacle course, but was he the strongest, too?

I hoped not. Andy was already obnoxious enough.

There was a brief delay, while the officials added another one-hundred-pound plate to each machine. The robots took their places once more, and Mr. Radnor gave them the go-ahead.

"Lift!" Yo and I shouted at SwiftBot in unison. He backed up a little slower this time, but his gait was steady. He pulled smoothly on the steel cable, gradually lifting all two hundred pounds from the mat. The ref raised his hand, and Yo and I grinned at each other.

So far, so good.

Next to us, MechaCrawler wasn't doing as well. Its metal feet scratched against the floor mats as it strained to pull itself forward a few feet more. The steel cable was stretched taut behind it, holding the stacked plates no more than three feet off the ground. "Please!" Persis urged her robot. "Keep going! Just a little higher!"

MechaCrawler pulled and pulled, but couldn't advance any farther. The air compressor in its shiny green thorax labored painfully. Ruptured pneumatic cylinders hissed like snakes. The two hundred pounds hovered above the floor, unable to rise all the way up. After ninety seconds, a ref blew her whistle, putting the exhausted robot out of its misery.

Persis and her robot had been eliminated from the weight lifting competition. She was stuck in fourth place again.

"That's too bad," I tried to console her. "MechaCrawler put up a good fight."

"Definitely," Yo agreed. "Don't forget. Even now, you're still number four in the whole country. That's not too shabby."

Persis sighed. "I suppose." She gazed mournfully at her defeated robot. "Thanks for saying so anyway."

Meanwhile, both RollerBot and FugBot had cleared the two hundred pounds as well. It was down to the three of us now.

"Hey, Spider-Chick!" Andy taunted Persis. He swaggered over from his own mat. "Why'd you even bother to show up anyway?"

"Shut up, Andy!" I warned him. Too bad he hadn't been eliminated instead of Persis. Andy's ego could use some deflating.

Mr. Radnor stepped between us. "That's enough, both of you. Let's keep this a friendly competition."

"Whatever," Andy muttered. He stomped back toward FugBot.

I hoped that he would leave Persis alone from now on. "Sorry about that," I said to Mr. Radnor. "You know how Andy can be."

"Too well," the science teacher admitted in a low voice. Every teacher at Shopton High had dealt with Andy at one time or another. "Just don't let him provoke you, okay? We've got an audience, remember."

Like I could forget the crowd and camera crews. "Got it."

Three hundred pounds were loaded onto the cable machines, and the competition resumed. SwiftBot was struggling now, but surrender was not in his programming. Step by step, he backed up across the mat as, inch by inch, the heavy iron plates rose from the base. Yo and I held our collective breath as the weights crept toward the five-foot mark. We gasped as SwiftBot staggered and missed a step. The plates dipped six inches or so, but the robot recovered and yanked the weights back up again. Precious seconds passed. I started to worry about whether we were going to run out of time.

Then, with a final tug, SwiftBot raised the plates the last few inches. The ref gave us the signal, and we breathed a sigh of relief.

Success!

I checked on the other robots. RollerBot had already completed the lift, but I was pleased to see that FugBot was having trouble. Leaning back so far that he was standing at a forty-five degree angle to the floor, the other humanoid robot had only managed to raise the iron plates by about three feet so far. His ebony arms and legs quivered from the strain.

"Keep going, you stupid machine!" Andy ordered his robot, visibly displeased by the 'bot's performance. His face was turning purple in rage. "Don't you dare give up on me!"

FugBot's time was running out, but he didn't even last the full ninety seconds. Without warning, the robot let go of the metal grip, releasing the cable. Three hundred pounds of solid iron crashed down onto the weight machine's base. The thunderous bang echoed throughout the gymnasium.

"Crud!" Andy grunted.

Remembering Mr. Radnor's advice, I resisted the temptation to gloat over FugBot's defeat. It was good to know, though, that Andy's robot was not completely unstoppable.

"Couldn't happen to a nicer guy," Yo said to me with a grin.

"You know it," I said.

With FugBot eliminated, the contest was between SwiftBot and RollerBot now. A full four hundred pounds was loaded onto our respective weight machines, and the final round began.

At first, the iron plates hardly budged. I winced in sympathy as SwiftBot's artificial muscles were put to the test. Yo gnawed nervously on a candy bar. Finally, with excruciating slowness, the weights started to creep upward.

One foot.

Two feet.

Two and a half . . .

It was agonizing to watch. "Maybe I should have wound another layer of muscle wire around his main armature," I whispered to Yo. "What if the tendons in his lower back can't take it?"

"Too late for second-guessing." She crossed her fingers. "We did what we could. Now it's up to SwiftBot."

To our right, RollerBot was slowly lifting the plates off their base. Synchronized motors whirred loudly as the one-armed robot pulled the steel cable taut. Three pairs of wheels rolled stubbornly across the mat until all four hundred pounds passed the five-foot mark.

"Yes!" Sue rejoiced. "You rule, girl!"

RollerBot had completed the lift. Now SwiftBot had to do the same, or the contest was over.

"C'mon, SwiftBot!" I urged the faltering robot. "Don't give up!"

"Go for it!" Yo shouted. "You're built to win!"

But, no matter how hard he strained, SwiftBot couldn't seem to raise the stacked plates any higher than four feet. The weights remained fixed at that height, unwilling to budge any farther. An internal monitor buzzed loudly, alerting us that the muscle wire was in danger of overheating. Too much current for too long, and the titanium strands would start to melt.

I exchanged an urgent look with Yo. "Well?"

She knew what I was asking. "No point wrecking him if he can't do it anyway. Pull the plug."

Left to his own programming, SwiftBot would keep trying to lift the weight until every metallic fiber in his body burned out. We didn't want that, though, not with one more event to go. Better to cut our losses while we still had a working robot.

"Stop," I instructed SwiftBot. "End routine."

He lowered the weights back down onto their base, then let go of the handlebar. The warning buzzer quieted down.

"Congratulations," I said to Sue Itami. "You won fair and square."

"Ditto," Yo agreed. "If I ever need a robot to do some heavy lifting, RollerBot is definitely at the top of my list!"

"Thanks!" Sue chirped. "You guys sure gave me a run for my money."

I took a second to review the score for the games so far. SwiftBot had come in second twice now, while

RollerBot and FugBot had each taken one first and one third. As a result, RollerBot, FugBot, and SwiftBot were all tied for first place in the overall competition, with one more event to go.

Talk about close! Whoever won the basketball competition, two days from now, was sure to claim the grand prize. It was a three-way race for the gold.

The one team that was out of the running was Persis and her MechaCrawler. Even if she took first place in the b-ball tournament, there was no way she could outscore the rest of us.

That had to be rough.

She was being a good sport about it, though. Joining us by RollerBot, she politely congratulated Sue while keeping her own disappointment to herself, unlike Andy, who stood several feet away, sulking, while Mr. Radnor announced the official results to the audience.

"And the winner, lifting an amazing four hundred pounds, is . . . RollerBot!"

7

Suspicions

The inside of SwiftBot's trailer looked like a high-tech operating room or, maybe, a mad scientist's laboratory. SwiftBot reclined atop an adjustable metal gurney, while Yo and I worked to get him ready for tomorrow's big basketball competition. I was replacing the springs in his feet. The rubber soles of his feet rested on a counter nearby. I had already removed the spent-uranium plugs we had used to increase his mass during the weight lifting competition. A thin plastic cable led from a socket in SwiftBot's neck to Yo's laptop. She pecked at her keyboard as she made some last-minute tweaks to his b-ball software. A biometric fingerprint reader guaranteed that no one else could open her files.

"I'm going to delete his weight lifting routines for the time being," she said. "That will free up more room in his hard drive for these new software patches." She nibbled on M&M's as she worked. "Plus, there will be less chance of the programs interfering with each other."

"Sounds good to me." I used a handheld tension meter to test the elasticity of the new springs, which were made of the same durable foam used in Formula One race cars. If there was time, I wanted to double-check the alignment of his infrared sensors as well, to make sure his depth perception was everything it should be. "Let's leave his track-and-field programs intact, though. He's going to need a lot of the same skills for playing hoops."

"Roger that," Yo said. Hip-hop music played over the trailer's sound system and she bobbed her head to the beat. "Running. Jumping. I can see that."

"FugBot has me worried," I admitted. "Remember how amazing Andy's robot was at the obstacle course?"

"It's burned into my brain too," Yo conceded. She scowled at the memory. "But, you know, basketball's not entirely the same thing. And we've spent mega-hours making SwiftBot a wizard on the court. Just think of all those practice sessions in your lab!"

Let's hope they paid off.

A knock at the trailer door interrupted my gloomy thoughts. I put down the used springs and went to the entrance. "Password?" I asked through the door.

"Give me a break!" Bud replied.

"That'll do." I threw open the door to let in Bud. He clambered into the trailer, a cardboard folder clasped beneath his arm. "So," I asked him, "what's this big news you couldn't just IM to us?"

"Oh, this is too major not to deliver in person." He sat down on a stool and nodded at Yo. "Hi, girl."

I could tell from his grin that he had dug up some good dirt. My curiosity hit a whole new level. "You found out who bugged all the trailers?"

"I wish!" he said. "That's still a mystery, but I did find out who that guy lurking outside FugBot's trailer was."

"Really?" Yo said, impressed. "How'd you manage that?"

He patted the folder on his lap. "I knew I'd seen that dude somewhere before, so I went digging through lots of old newspaper archives. Look what I found." He opened the folder and pulled out several pages of printouts from various news sites. One of the headlines instantly caught my eye:

OLYMPIC STAR QUITS IN DISGRACE
Robertson Fails Drug Test

Beneath the headline was a color photo of the guy we had surprised two nights ago. I recognized his curly red hair and bushy mustache instantly, not to mention the shifty look in his eyes.

"Right!" I said, snapping my fingers. "I remember this guy now. Jay Robertson. He was a big-deal Olympic athlete who got caught in a steroids scandal. It was all over the news a few years back."

"Oh yeah. It's coming back to me," Yo said. "Wasn't he expected to win the decathlon at the 2004 Olympics in Athens, before he got busted?" A puzzled expression came over her face. "So what was he doing outside FugBot's trailer the other night? Robots don't need steroids."

"Well, we can probably rule out Andy's lame watchman explanation," I decided. "You don't need a disgraced Olympian just to babysit a sleeping robot."

Bud scratched his chin. "Maybe Andy hired Robertson to help him train FugBot. Give him some pointers on how FugBot should move and all. That's not against the rules, is it?"

"No," I admitted. In theory Andy even could have used some sort of motion-capture system to record Robertson's movements and program them into Fug-Bot, kind of like when Hollywood uses a real actor as a model for a computer-generated monster or alien. "But then why all the secrecy? Why should Robertson care if we saw him?"

"I haven't spotted him at any of the events," Yo pointed out. "Not in the audience and not with Andy on the floor. If Robertson is coaching FugBot some-how, how come he's never around when FugBot's competing?"

"Maybe Robertson just wants to keep a low pro-file," Bud suggested. As usual, his common sense got in the way of a really good conspiracy theory. "After all the bad press he got a few years back, I can see where he might want to avoid being in the spotlight again. The Fogers probably aren't all that keen on being associated with a loser like Robertson either. Even if it's technically legal, it still looks bad. I mean, think about it. The headlines practically write themselves: 'OLYMPIC CHEATER COACHES ROBO ATHLETE.'" He whistled at the thought. "No wonder Robertson's hiding out in FugBot's trailer, away from the cameras."

"I suppose," I said grudgingly. "But knowing Andy, I can't help thinking that he and Robertson are up to something fishy." I still suspected Andy of being involved with the buggings as well, even though Robertson and the guy in the ski mask couldn't possibly be the same person.

Where did Ski Mask fit into the picture? Or was there no connection at all?

8

Hoops

The backboard shattered. Fragments of Plexiglas rained down onto the gym floor, along with the bright orange basketball that had done the damage.

"Oops!" Sue Itami blurted. "My bad! Guess Roller-Bot doesn't know her own strength."

The robot in question was unfazed by the accident. She and SwiftBot moved aside to let some Robo Olympics volunteers hustle onto the court to clean up the mess.

Too bad the backboard wasn't made of SwiftGlass. "Hey, Q.U.I.P. Remind me to have SE donate some unbreakable backboards to the school, okay?"

"Sure thing," my wristwatch replied. "I'll give you a nudge when things quiet down."

Right now, of course, I had other things on my mind. The spectacular destruction of the backboard had interrupted the first match in the basketball minitournament, the final event of the Robot Olympics. A random drawing had pitted SwiftBot against RollerBot in a one-on-one game of half-court hoops, with FugBot and MechaCrawler facing off in the next match. The winners of the two preliminary matches would compete against each other for first place.

With the top three robots all tied for first in the overall standings, the basketball competition had drawn a huge audience. The gym bleachers were packed with spectators, including Sandy and my parents, while the live-TV coverage was expected to generate astronomical ratings. Bud was just one of an entire mob of reporters crammed into the press area. One way or another, the outcome of the Robo Olympics would be determined today.

"RollerBot packs quite a punch," Yo commented.

"Looks like it," I said, "but scoring in hoops takes a more delicate touch."

As we watched the volunteers hastily replace the backboard, I recalled my practice games with

SwiftBot back at my lab. In many ways, basketball was the ultimate test of the robots' strength, speed, skill, and smarts. People sometimes called b-ball a mental game, and they weren't kidding. A good player has to be able to keep track of the ball, his opponent, and his own position, all at the same time. It was about sizing up a situation on the run and figuring out what to do next, usually with only seconds to spare. Lifting a heavy load, or managing an obstacle course, was kid stuff compared to playing hoops at a competitive level.

SwiftBot joined us on the sidelines. A special adhesive mat removed any loose dust, dirt, or wax from the rubber soles of his feet. *Every little bit helps*, I thought. Keeping the soles clean would give Swift-Bot better traction.

Once the new backboard was in place, the game started up again. SwiftBot was awarded possession of the ball and quickly went on the offensive. RollerBot played defense, blocking SwiftBot's approach to the free-throw lane. Dribbling with both hands, the humanoid robot tried to dodge past RollerBot, but the wheeled robot could turn surprisingly fast when she had to. Zipping back and forth across the court,

RollerBot kept between SwiftBot and the basket.

The score stood at 10-9 in our favor. Baskets counted for one point, except when thrown from beyond the three-point line, which was more than twenty feet away from the basket. In a one-on-one game like this one, that counted for two points. Eleven points won the game, provided there was a two-point margin at the end.

SwiftBot needed only one more point to win.

Retreating backward, almost to the three-point line, our robot dropped into the triple-threat stance. He faked to the left, then launched a long shot at the basket.

The orange sphere arced from SwiftBot's mechanical fingertips. The trajectory looked perfect, right on track to score. The crowd held its breath. Was this it, the winning basket?

Nope.

RollerBot's single arm telescoped upward, doubling in length. The extended arm blocked the shot, and sent the ball ricocheting away from the basket.

"Arrgh!" Yo growled. She tugged on her hair in frustration.

We were so close to winning!

"Neat trick," I said to Sue, who was standing with us on the sidelines.

"Thanks!" she replied. "I programmed RollerBot to save it for an emergency."

On the court, SwiftBot scrambled after the ball, trying to regain possession before the ball bounced out of bounds. He snagged it only inches from the midcourt line and dribbled it back toward the hoop.

Good save, I thought, admiring his technique. Sensors in his fingertips provided the feedback he needed to gauge the amount of pressure he exerted on the ball. Rubber pads helped him maintain his grip. Not exactly the "hot hands" prized by NBA champions, but it would have to do.

He charged the free-throw lane. Wheels squealing, RollerBot zoomed to block him, her super-size arm waving back and forth in the air like a metronome.

"Jump!" I shouted over the roar of the crowd. Even with RollerBot's extendable arm, SwiftBot still had a definite height advantage.

RollerBot's low center of gravity, which had lent her stability during the obstacle course, worked against her here. As the hurdle challenge had demonstrated before, the tanklike robot was not much of a jumper.

Unlike SwiftBot.

"Go for it!" Yo yelled. "Jump!"

I had no idea if he could hear us, but SwiftBot vaulted into the air, holding the ball high above his head with his left arm, which could shoot just as well as his right. That was one advantage robots had over us human types. SwiftBot was built to be ambidextrous. He waited until he reached the very top of his ascent, then propelled the ball toward the basket in a near-perfect skyhook.

The ball swished through the hoop and the game was over. Cheers erupted from the audience. SwiftBot beat RollerBot, 11 to 9.

Sue took the defeat well. "That's the way the ball bounces, I guess."

Yo and I groaned at the bad joke.

"Seriously," she added. "Congratulations, dudes." She gave us a mock salute. "To be honest, I never expected to score big at b-ball. That's a sport better suited to humans—or robots shaped like humans. My big strategy for winning the Robo Olympics depended on RollerBot taking first place in both the

obstacle run and the weight lifting." She sighed rue-
fully. "FugBot sure messed up that plan!"

I remembered how Andy's robot had outshone us
all at the first event. "Don't remind me!"

Sue stepped closer and lowered her voice. "Do me
a favor, guys," she whispered. "If you get the chance,
stomp FugBot and Andy into the ground. Don't let
that loudmouth jerk win the grand prize!"

"Trust me," I said. "That's the last thing any of us
wants."

Pretty soon, it looked like we were taking on Andy for
sure. The second preliminary match had barely started,
and FugBot was already beating MechaCrawler, 9-5.
Yo and I watched from the bleachers as Andy's robot
went for yet another score. He sprang explosively
into the air and, with a flick of his wrist, rolled the
ball off his fingers. To my horror, I saw that FugBot
had actually put a bit of backspin on the ball, a trick
that was still beyond SwiftBot's abilities.

The spin on the ball proved its worth as the
leather sphere hit the rim of the basket. Instead of
bouncing away at an angle, it dropped straight
through the hoop, bringing the score to 10-5.

"Did you see that?" Andy crowed from the sidelines. "FugBot's a scoring machine. That stupid spider is going down, big-time!"

Persis winced at Andy's remarks, but she didn't say anything.

I scanned the crowd but couldn't spot Jay Robertson anywhere in the gymnasium. Where was the disgraced sports star hiding, and why wasn't he here for the big event?

The Robo Olympics rules called for loser's outs, so FugBot's basket granted MechaCrawler possession. With eight limbs, the robotic spider was great at dribbling, but not so hot at scoring. It bounced the ball from limb to limb, successfully keeping it out of FugBot's reach, while it scuttled toward the hoop. As soon as it was within range, it lifted the ball up above its thorax and batted it at the basket. FugBot leaped to block it but tripped over another of MechaCrawler's legs. The ball soared through air—only to miss the basket completely.

Air ball!

Persis stared at her feet. She looked like she wanted to be anywhere else at the moment.

Recovering from his stumble, FugBot crashed the

boards in pursuit of the loose ball. He quickly brought it under control and sprinted down the court, going in for the kill. MechaCrawler cut across the key to intercept its opponent. It lifted half of its spidery limbs in the air in order to create as much of an obstacle as possible. A front leg tried to snatch the ball away from FugBot, but the glossy black robot was way too agile for that. FugBot effortlessly dribbled the ball behind his back and between his legs, keeping the "rock" one bounce away from the other robot. "Wow," I muttered.

How *had* Andy pulled that off? Even if his father's scientists had helped him build the robot, FugBot's smooth moves were depressingly awesome.

"Shake and bake!" he yelled at his robot. "Leave that bug in the dust!"

FugBot moved like a pro, darting around the spider-bot. With a clear path to the basket, he ran right up to the net and blasted off from the floor. His lightweight plastic shell seemed to lend him an unbelievable amount of hang time. Suspended in the air, above the basket, he jammed the ball through the hoop with both hands.

Slam dunk!

With that FugBot easily won the match, 11-5. MechaCrawler never even had a chance.

Guess Sue was right. Humanoid robots really did have the edge in basketball.

"Congra—," Persis began, but Andy ignored her.

He gave Yolanda and me an evil grin. "You're next, Swift!"

Our respective victories meant that FugBot and SwiftBot would face off for first place. First, however, RollerBot and MechaCrawler had to compete against each other to determine who came in third and fourth in the basketball tournament.

"What a waste of time!" Andy groused. "Who wants to see these losers play? I'm going to get something to eat." He stomped off toward the exit. "Let me know when it's time for the *real* event."

Your loss, I thought. Even though I was primed for the final match, too, a battle between the two non-humanoid robots was too interesting to ignore. This time neither opponent had the advantage of a human shape. I was curious to see which came out ahead, wheels or spider legs?

"Bet you a pizza MechaCrawler wins," Yo challenged me. "I've got a feeling about that bug."

"You're on!" I told her.

After several minutes of play it became clear that, for once, MechaCrawler was the robot to beat. RollerBot was faster, but the mechanical insect monopolized the ball. RollerBot chased in circles around MechaCrawler but could never catch up with the ball. About the only time Sue's robot got possession was after MechaCrawler scored another point. RollerBot had to shoot fast every time she got her hand on the ball, or risk having it stolen away by one of the robotic spider's many limbs.

Both robots made more shots than they missed. Soon the score was 11-10 in MechaCrawler's favor. Even though the spider-bot already had eleven points, it still needed one more basket to beat Roller-Bot by the required two-point margin. At that point it was still any robot's game.

"You're almost there!" Sue cheered for her robot. "Just a few more points!"

Momentarily in possession of the ball once more, RollerBot wasted no time scooting beyond the three-point line. Her single arm dribbled the ball against the floor as she spun around on her rear wheels to position herself for the shot. MechaCrawler came scurrying at her like an oversize tarantula, so RollerBot rushed a hook shot over the defender's waving limbs.

"That's my girl!" Sue shouted in encouragement. "Bring it home, baby!"

A few feet away, Persis mouthed something as well, but her voice was too soft to be heard over the crowd. I assumed she was rooting for her own robot.

The ball flew in a sweeping arc above the court. MechaCrawler didn't pause to see if RollerBot made the shot. Instead it scuttled back toward the hoop, hoping to nab the rebound if the ball missed its target. RollerBot sped after the defender, just as intent on getting ready for whatever happened next.

"Come on, come on . . . ," Sue pleaded. "Bury that rock!"

But RollerBot's haste spoiled her accuracy. The ball smacked against the backboard and bounced back down onto the court. It hit the floor between the two robots, then bounded past RollerBot. The wheeled robot spun around so fast she left skid marks on the hardwood floor, and she managed to get to the unclaimed ball first. She blocked it with her front bumper, slowing the ball down long enough for her single arm to swivel around and grab on to it. Throwing the ball against the floor, she dribbled the ball in front of her.

"Shoot!" Sue yelled. "Shoot!"

MechaCrawler didn't give RollerBot a chance to make another basket. A pneumatic limb swept out and snagged the ball as it was bouncing back up from the floor. Before RollerBot could react, MechaCrawler passed the rock along to its rear limbs, just like a one-robot assembly line. The back limbs hoisted the ball into the air, then catapulted it at the basket.

The bank shot hit the backboard at just the right angle. *Ba-boom!* The ball bounced off the Plexiglas into the basket.

"And the winner is . . . MechaCrawler!" Mr. Radnor announced.

"Oh . . . wow!" Persis exclaimed. She looked like she couldn't believe her ears.

The win meant that MechaCrawler came in third in the basketball tournament. Unfortunately, beating

RollerBot was not enough to lift her out of fourth place in the overall standings. Too little, too late.

But I was glad that Persis hadn't been totally skunked.

"Hah!" Yo laughed. She grinned at me triumphantly, having won our bet. "You owe me a pizza, sucker."

"You called it," I admitted. "Your usual? Canadian bacon and pineapple?"

"What else?"

Sue sighed and offered Persis her hand. "Good game!" she said enthusiastically. "Eight arms are clearly better than one."

Persis tried to wave away Sue's praise. "Even if I'm still coming in last in the games as a whole?"

"Even if!" Sue insisted. "Besides, there's always next year."

"Maybe." Persis's expression darkened and a funny tone entered her voice. "If there is a next year."

Huh? What did she mean by that?

Finally, it was time for the main event. FugBot versus SwiftBot. One-on-one. With first place in the Robot Olympics at stake.

"This is it," Yo said nervously. She paced back and forth along the sidelines, gnawing on a Tootsie Roll. "I just hope my nerves can take it."

"SwiftBot's as ready as he'll ever be," I said confidently. "I know we can count on your software at least."

Andy interrupted my pep talk. "You're fooling yourself, Swift. FugBot is going to wipe up the floor with your pathetic tin man."

I refused to let him intimidate me. "We'll see about that."

A whistle blew and the game began.

FugBot started out strong, piling up an impressive lead. Within minutes the score was 8-1 in his favor. *This doesn't look good*, I thought. Frustration churned inside me. Yo and I had worked too hard to settle for second place. I hated the idea of losing to Andy of all people.

But then things started going our way. FugBot seemed to be slowing down as the game progressed, like he was running out of steam. Weak batteries? I remembered how FugBot had given out abruptly during the weight lifting contest. Maybe the speedy black robot wasn't built for the long haul?

In that case SwiftBot might just be able to outlast him. He had endurance to spare.

"Keep it up!" I cheered for our robot. "You got game!"

Pretty soon, we had nearly evened out the score. At 9-8, SwiftBot played the post, looking to nail another basket. He dribbled the ball with both hands, while FugBot stubbornly kept between our robot and the hoop. His arms and elbows extended outward, blocking SwiftBot's path to the zone. No way was he going to let the other robot past him.

Andy's robot had a definite height advantage. At over six feet, with proportional arms, FugBot had a standing reach of nearly eight feet. And unlike RollerBot, he could jump just as high as SwiftBot, if not higher. Getting past his aggressive defense would not be easy.

Ball in hands, SwiftBot turned his head and shoulders toward the right. Yo and I exchanged a glance as we recognized his fake-out technique. Would the other robot fall for it?

FugBot darted to his left to block him, just like SwiftBot wanted him to. Yes! Before Andy's robot could figured out that he'd been tricked, SwiftBot pivoted back toward the basket and fired off a hook shot.

"Gotcha" I yelled.

Yo gave me a high-five. "I *knew* that fake-out subroutine was worth all the trouble it gave me!"

The ball dipped toward the hoop. Realizing what was up, FugBot spun around and leaped after the ball, desperately trying to block it in time. Black plastic fingers batted the ball away from the basket right before it dropped through the net.

"Foul!" The ref—Couch Jenkins—blew his whistle. It was against the rules to interfere with the ball once it was over the rim. "Goaltending!" Coach Jenkins declared. A former pro baseball player, Shopton High's favorite PE teacher was serving as referee for the match. He was a tall African American man in his late forties, with broad shoulders and a crew cut. "Free throw to SwiftBot."

"What!" Andy shouted. His face turned red. "You're kidding me!"

"You arguing with me, Foger?" the Coach challenged him.

Andy knew better than to contest the ruling. "No," he muttered sourly.

Needless to say, Yo and I were thrilled to be awarded the foul shot. "This could be the break we need," I said. "SwiftBot is great at free throws."

"He's better than great!" she said. "He couldn't miss this if he tried."

Knock on wood.

SwiftBot took his place at the free-throw line, only fifteen feet away from the backboard. FugBot stood by helplessly, prohibited from interfering with the throw.

"Take your time!" I urged our robot. "You can do it!"

"Bury that rock!" Yo shouted.

Andy glowered at us.

SwiftBot raised the ball before him, took aim, . . . and scored!

The audience roared in approval. The game was now even, 9-9. Both robots needed only two more points to win the match, the tournament, and the entire Robot Olympics.

We were down to the wire. The next few minutes would determine everything. It was do or die.

Andy knew that too. "Don't let me down, you stupid robot!"

Regaining possession of the ball, FugBot shake-and-baked, trying to get past SwiftBot. The silver robot hustled to box him out, sticking to his opponent as though they were magnetized together. Black plastic grazed silver carbon fiber as they jostled each other. SwiftBot's arm reached for the ball again and again, aiming to steal the rock, but FugBot was too crafty for that. Andy's robot dribbled the ball behind his back to keep it out of SwiftBot's eager clutches.

"Yikes!" Yo exclaimed. "I hate to say it, but that robot's got some killer moves."

"There are *people* who can't dribble that well," I admitted.

Turning his back on the defender, FugBot sprinted past the three-point line. My heart pounded. If the ebony robot made a two-point basket from outside the line, the match was over.

"Stop him!" I yelled to SwiftBot. "Don't let him score!"

SwiftBot raced to get in his opponent's way. Fug-Bot crouched low, then sprang into the air. His right arm carried the ball aloft before releasing it into the air. SwiftBot rocketed up to block the shot but couldn't get enough altitude. I stared in horror as the ball soared above SwiftBot's outstretched fingers. Yo gasped and threw her hands over her mouth.

It was a perfect jump shot. The ball came down right on target, touching nothing but net.

FugBot had won, 11-9.

"All right!" Andy exclaimed. "Game over!"

That's that, I thought. The Robot Olympics were all wrapped up. As the adrenaline rush faded, a numb feeling came over me. The final awards ceremony, attended by Dr. VanderMeer would not be until tomorrow morning, but I could calculate the ultimate results easily enough.

Fourth place: MechaCrawler.

Third place: RollerBot.

Second place: SwiftBot.

First place: FugBot!

"I can't believe it," Yo groaned. "We lost . . . to Andy."

Talk about adding insult to injury. "We're never going to hear the end of this."

"Starting now, it looks like," she said.

Andy swaggered over to us. "See!" he gloated.

Smug self-satisfaction was written all over his beefy face. "Didn't I tell you that FugBot would clobber your wimpy robot? How's it feel to know you're only second-best?"

Not so hot.

9

Follow That Car!

"Thanks for giving me a lift home," my sister said. She leaned back against the passenger seat of the Speedster as we cruised through Shopton with the top down. A warm breeze blew past our heads. "I can't wait until I have wheels of my own."

"No problem," I told her. Our parents were having dinner with some old scientist friends who were in town for the Robot Olympics, but neither Sandy nor I were in the mood to listen to lots of grown-up chatter and reminiscences all night. After tucking Swift-Bot away in his trailer, I just wanted to go home and veg out for the evening. Tomorrow's final awards ceremony was going to come all too soon as it was. "I've got nothing better to do."

Sandy must have heard how discouraged I sounded. "Sorry SwiftBot lost the big game," she said. "You almost won. Plus, second place in the whole Robo Olympics thing is nothing to sneeze at."

"I guess." I appreciated Sandy's efforts to cheer me up, but I was still feeling pretty down. Yo had taken off with Bud to drown her sorrows in a hot-fudge sundae. I had been tempted to join them but had decided that I'd rather be by myself for a while. Maybe I would get back to work on that jetpack. Get my mind off robots until tomorrow.

Sandy peered into the passenger-side mirror, then glanced back over her shoulder. "Heads up, big brother," she said. "Don't look now, but I think we're being followed."

"What?" I started to turn around in my seat.

Sandy punched me in the shoulder. "I said, *don't look!*"

I peeked in the rearview mirror instead. "Which car?"

"The white sedan," she informed me. She rifled through the handbag on her lap and extracted a small cosmetic case. Flipping open the compact, she used its mirror to keep watch on the other car while pretending to check her makeup. "I'm not a hundred-percent certain, but I'm pretty sure it's been dogging our tail since we left the school."

I spotted the car she meant, a snow white sedan. It was about two cars behind us and one lane over. As far as I knew, I had never seen it before.

"Let's check this out," I said. Even though we were only a few miles away from our house, I made some random turns that carried us away from the suburbs and deeper into Shopton's business district. The rush-hour traffic grew heavier as we veered left at the bowling alley and headed straight down Stratemeyer Avenue. Department stores, office buildings, and coffee shops lined the busy thoroughfare. "Well?" I asked Sandy after a few minutes. "He still with us?"

Sandy tilted her mirror to get a better look. "Yep. A few cars back." She grinned broadly, sounding more excited than concerned about our mysterious shadow. "This is awesome! For once, I'm not missing out on all the action!"

My sister was convinced that she always got the short end of the stick just because she was one year younger than me. She was still kicking herself for having missed all that excitement outside the trailers the other night. The truth is, I think I'm just better at getting into tight spots than she is. "Lucky you," I replied.

I stared into the rearview mirror, trying to get a look at the driver of the sedan. All I could make out was a male figure behind the wheel. A baseball cap and mirrored sunglasses helped disguise the driver's identity. He could have been almost anybody.

Who? I wondered.

Jay Robertson, the disgraced Olympian?

A TRB terrorist or sympathizer?

The guy in the ski mask who bugged our trailer?

Somebody else altogether?

"Who could it be?" Sandy asked eagerly. Her gaze was glued to the mirror of her compact. "What do you think he's after?"

"Beats me," I confessed. My brain raced as I tried to figure out what to do next. I could always contact the police or SE Security via Q.U.I.P., but that might just scare our shadow away before we could find out who he was. I didn't want to just lose our pursuer—I wanted some answers, too. After a few more turns, an idea struck me. "I think I know how to turn the tables on him, if we can just get out of his sight for a few minutes."

Sandy pounced on the challenge. "I know just the trick!" She glanced around at the street signs as we continued to drive through downtown. "Okay, we just passed the intersection of Thirty-fifth and Waverly. There should be an alley coming up on your right, about two blocks from here, that connects with Pine Avenue."

I took her word for it. Sandy had a photographic memory, and she had long since memorized the local maps. When it came to getting around Shopton and the surrounding areas, she was more reliable than a state-of-the-art GPS system.

Sure enough, the alley she mentioned popped up right in front of us. I mentally apologized to my old driver's-ed instructor as, without signaling first, I made a sharp right turn into the alley. The narrow passage-way looked clear ahead, so I hit the gas to increase the distance between us and the sedan. The sudden accel-eration tossed Sandy back against her seat. "Hey!" she protested. "A little warning next time!"

I glanced in the mirror. The sedan hadn't entered the alley yet, which meant there was still time to pull a fast one on our pursuer. If I couldn't see him, then he couldn't see us. . . .

"Attention: SW-1," I said loudly. "Execute external modifications. Model number . . . 16/B."

The Speedster immediately responded to my voice commands. Its nanoplastic shell reshaped itself in a matter of minutes. Millions of tiny molecular machines flowed upward, forming a top over our heads. The flashy sports car morphed into a retro-looking coupe. Even the color of the car's exterior changed, going from cherry red to midnight blue. Tinted windows hid our faces.

"Talk about an extreme makeover!" Sandy exclaimed. "You have *got* to build me one of these for my birthday next year!"

By the time we reached the end of the alley, the transformation was complete. I peeked in the mirror: still no sign of the sedan. Maybe he had missed the turn and had to double back? *Good*, I thought. That meant he didn't see the car change its appearance.

We pulled out onto Pine Avenue and waited to see if the white sedan followed us out of the alley. Thirty seconds later, there it was, right on schedule. An oncoming car honked angrily as the sedan hastily forced its way onto Pine. I couldn't make out our shadow's face anymore, but boy, was he in for a surprise! It wasn't hard to imagine his confused expression as he looked around frantically for the bright red sports car he had been following.

"Tough luck, creep," I said. "You've been punk'd!"

"Way to go, bro!" Sandy gave me a high five. "Now what?"

I slowed down and let the sedan pass us. The driver didn't even give us a second look.

"Now we do to him," I told her, "what he was doing to us. Follow him and see where he goes."

The sedan circled around the block a couple of times, no doubt searching for the red Speedster, before finally giving up. We kept a safe distance behind the other car as it drove back toward the school. I didn't think the driver spotted us following him, but if he tried to shake us, I figured I'd just change the Speedster's appearance again to fool him. Given all the different models and colors I had programmed into the car's memory, we could probably trail him halfway across the country without being spotted.

Not that he was going that far.

"Think he's going back to our school?" Sandy asked. "He's heading that way."

"Maybe," I said, "but I'm not sure why. There's nothing else going on there until tomorrow."

As it turned out the sedan wasn't going to Shopton High after all. It continued on the road past the school until it reached a hotel a few miles farther ahead. I watched the white car pull into the hotel's parking lot. "Must be from out of town," I guessed.

I didn't pull into the hotel lot myself. We didn't want to spook him by following too closely. Instead I parked across the street in front of a convenience store. "Quick!" I said to Sandy. "There are binoculars in the glove compartment. Hand them over, pronto!"

Sandy passed the binoculars over in a hurry.

Peering through the magnifying lenses, I spotted the sedan parking in an empty space. My eyes widened as the driver exited his vehicle and took a moment to stretch his limbs. His scowling face suggested that he was still unhappy about losing us back at the alley. Thinking he was unobserved, he removed his cap and shades.

I recognized his blow-dried hair and photogenic profile immediately.

"Whoa!" I blurted. "It's Luke McCabe!"

"Who?" Sandy asked.

"This cable news guy who's been covering the games."

"Weird!" she said. "I don't get it. Why would he be following you now?"

"Good question. I'm stumped," I said. It was better, I supposed, to have a reporter following you than a terrorist, but that still left plenty of unanswered questions. I wondered if McCabe and Ski Mask were the same guy. Was the reporter the prowler who had tried to bug all the trailers a few nights ago?

"This doesn't make any sense," I complained. "The Robo Olympics are all but over, so what's his angle?" I put down the binoculars and scratched my head in confusion. "And why me? I don't have anything to hide, and I'm not going to win the grand prize. Andy Foger is."

So why isn't McCabe tailing Andy instead?

My first instinct was to call out McCabe right there and then. I was going to storm right up to the reporter's hotel room, pound on his door, and find out why he was tailing me. But when I checked with the front desk, a clerk told me that there was no "Luke McCabe" checked into the hotel. I tried describing McCabe, but the snooty clerk wasn't terribly helpful. "I'm afraid we cannot give out any sort of information concerning our guests," he explained.

He had a point, I guess. It wasn't like I was an FBI agent or something. Why should he help a kid my age track down some guy I'd just seen in the parking lot out front? The more I thought about it, the flimsier my case seemed. Even if I knew what room McCabe was in, there was nothing illegal about a journalist following someone in public. If it were, half the paparazzi in Hollywood would be behind bars. I didn't have any sort of restraining order out against McCabe.

"Let's go home," I told Sandy. It had been a long, draining day and I was ready for it to be over. Whatever McCabe was up to could wait until tomorrow. Maybe I would run into him at the awards ceremony.

Our parents were still out when Sandy and I got home. I tinkered around in my lab for a while, answered some e-mails and IMs, then went to bed early.

But as the hours dragged by, I found it hard to sleep. Even when I managed to doze off for a while, I had anxiety dreams about showing up for the awards ceremony five hours late. Then I dreamed SwiftBot blamed me for his defeat because I had opted to give him a silvery finish. "No wonder I came in second every time!" he accused me, even though he didn't have a speech synthesizer. "You made me the color of a second-place medal!"

I woke up around six, then couldn't get back to sleep. After tossing and turning for a while, I finally gave up and got out of bed. The sun had not risen and the house was eerily quiet. Even the cleaning 'bots were recharging in their nooks.

Restless, I decided to head over to the trailer and spruce up SwiftBot for the ceremony later that morning. He had picked up some dings and scratches during the b-ball matches and could use a good polish. I figured he might as well look good for the TV cameras even if he wasn't coming in first place.

Just so my parents wouldn't worry, I instructed our house's message center to tell them that I had left early for the ceremony.

To confuse any would-be shadows, the Speedster now resembled a bronze-colored station wagon. Even still, I kept checking the rearview mirror as I drove, watching out for any suspicious vehicles that seemed to be deliberately going my way. There was no sign of McCabe's white sedan, however, or anybody else tailing me. *Careful*, I warned myself. *You don't want to be getting all paranoid now.*

So what if McCabe was investigating me? I had nothing to hide.

The sun was just breaking through the clouds when I arrived at Shopton High. As I pulled into the parking lot, my jaw dropped at the sight of a white sedan parked in front of the school.

Huh? What was McCabe doing here already at this ridiculous hour? The big awards ceremony didn't start until ten a.m., nearly three hours from now. Don't tell me he showed up this early just to get a good parking spot.

I didn't like the look of this.

Parking the Speedster in its usual space, I crept toward the fenced-in area where the robots' trailers were being kept. Chances were, that's where McCabe had headed, especially if the reporter and Ski Mask were one and the same as I was really starting to suspect. I figured I should alert the guards that he was around.

But as I approached the gate, I was surprised to see

the reporter talking with the guards himself. On a hunch, I ducked behind a streetlight so neither the uniforms nor McCabe would see me. Better safe than sorry.

They were too far away for me to hear what they were saying. I wished I had my parabolic microphone on me. Then I could have eavesdropped on the men from a distance.

Suddenly, the guards stepped aside to let McCabe enter the trailer lot. What kind of security was that? I realized that the guards had to be working with the reporter for some reason. That was the only explanation.

McCabe disappeared into the lot while the guards remained at their post. I waited a few minutes, then approached the gate myself. "Hi there." I greeted them casually, trying to pretend like everything was totally normal. "You guys still holding down the fort?"

"You're here awful early," one of the men commented. "Shouldn't you still be in bed?" Was it only my imagination, or were the guards less than happy to see me?

"Couldn't sleep," I said, honestly enough. "And my robot needs to get cleaned up for today's show."

The two men hesitated, like they were trying to think of an excuse to turn me away, but hey, I was the second-place winner in the Robot Olympics. Why shouldn't I be allowed to see my own robot?

They stepped aside and I strolled through the gate. I kept acting all casual, until I was out of sight of the guards. Then I crouched over and started sneaking through the lot as quietly as I could. With luck, I could creep up on McCabe and catch him red-handed at whatever he was up to. At this point, I was willing to bet Yo a dozen pizzas that the reporter and Ski Mask were the same person, but I still had no clue what he was after.

Why would McCabe be snooping around the trailers now? The games were over. It was too late to spy on or sabotage the competition. So what was his motive?

I kept to the shadows, avoiding the glare of the streetlights. One of these days, I really needed to get around to building that stealth invisibility suit I had been thinking about for months. The idea was simple enough: Focus a camera on the scene behind you, then project that image onto the front of a suit composed of hundreds of tiny glass beads. The beads would reflect the image back to any viewer, who would end up "seeing through" you. Unfortunately, the concept still hadn't gotten any further than some sketches and diagrams in my laptop. I could have used a suit like that right now.

First I checked on SwiftBot's trailer, which seemed to be undisturbed. Same for FugBot's trailer, not that I really cared all that much. Manga-style cartoons of Sue and RollerBot decorated the outside of their trailer. I was just checking the padlock on their door, when I heard a metallic scratching sound coming from a few yards away.

What's that?

Moving silently, I peered around the corner of RollerBot's trailer. By now, the sky had lightened enough that I could see McCabe picking the lock on MechaCrawler's trailer. He fumbled with the lock for a few moments, then pulled open the door and darted inside the trailer. The door clicked shut behind him.

No way! I thought angrily. Trying to follow me

home was one thing. Breaking and entering into Persis's private trailer was crossing the line. Persis had gone through enough at these games. The last thing she needed was some crooked reporter poking around where he didn't belong!

There was no point in calling the guards. They were obviously working with McCabe. I was going to have to deal with him on my own.

Fine, I thought. This time McCabe wasn't going to be able to hide behind a hotel desk clerk or escape over a fence. I remembered landing on my butt in Ski Mask's instant oil slick and got even more ticked off. My fists clenched at my sides. One way or another, I was going to get some answers from Luke McCabe before he could get away again.

The door was still unlocked, so I yanked it open and rushed inside the trailer. "Gotcha!" I shouted, hoping to startle him. "Mind telling me just what you think you're doing here?"

But the reporter didn't answer. Instead he lay unconscious on the floor of the trailer, silent and unmoving. Fluorescent lights overhead revealed MechaCrawler standing over McCabe's body. An air compressor hummed within the spider-bot's thorax.

Pneumatic limbs hissed ominously. A sonar range finder locked onto me.

"Huh?" I blurted. "What the—"

A metal leg lashed out at my head.

Everything went dark.

10

The Truth Comes Out

Who knows how long I was out. Gradually, though, my brain rebooted itself and I started to come to. It took me a minute to remember where I was, but then it all came back to me. The last thing I recalled was MechaCrawler attacking me.

Talk about a sore loser!

A groan escaped my lips. My head felt like, well, it had just been whacked by a giant mechanical spider. Groggily, I opened my eyes. Everything was blurry at first, but the view slowly came into focus. Too bad I didn't like what I saw.

I found myself on the floor of the trailer, staring up at the ceiling. Metal cables were wrapped around

my chest, pinning my arms to my side. Another set of cables tied my ankles together. I tried to wriggle free of the metal cords, but they were wrapped around me too tightly.

"Aww, man," I muttered. Like a fly caught in a spider's web, I wasn't going anywhere soon.

"Are you all right, Tom?" a concerned voice asked.

Turning my head, I saw Luke McCabe lying on the floor next to me. His arms and legs were also bound. An ugly purple bruise covered his forehead.

Wait a second. If the reporter was a prisoner, too, then who . . . ?

"Sorry I can't offer either of you a chair," a soft voice said, "but I wasn't really expecting company."

I recognized the voice right away. "Persis?"

The thin, shy girl stood a few feet away, in front of a stainless-steel work counter. MechaCrawler crouched beside her, guarding the closed door of the trailer.

"There's no point in calling for help," she warned us. "The walls of this trailer are one-hundred-percent soundproof to keep spies from listening in on me." She gave McCabe a dirty look. "Apparently, that didn't stop certain people from snooping anyway."

Did she think I was with McCabe? "You don't understand," I said. "I was trying to stop McCabe from getting at your stuff!"

She shook her head sadly. "That doesn't matter now. I can't risk letting either of you go before I've completed my mission."

Now I was completely confused. "Mission?"

"Ask your friend, the FBI agent," Persis said snarkily. She held up a badge in a leather holder. "I took this off him while you were unconscious."

My head was spinning. FBI? "What's this all about?"

"She's TRB," McCabe spit out harshly. "An anti-science terrorist."

"What!" Persis . . . a member of The Road Back? "Are you serious?"

"It's true," he insisted. "The news job is just a cover. We'd heard a rumor that TRB had infiltrated one of the teams competing in these games. We just didn't know which one." Frustration added a bitter edge to his voice. "That's why I tried bugging all the trailers."

McCabe's story sounded plausible enough. No

wonder the guards at the gate let him into the lot. He must have flashed his badge at them, then asked them to keep quiet about it.

"I'm not a terrorist," Persis said fervently. "I'm a defender of humanity, fighting to save the planet from being overrun by mechanical monsters!"

"Like the one you built?" I accused her. My head was still sore from where MechaCrawler had walloped me.

Persis shrugged. "Sometimes you have to fight fire with fire," she said. "Can I help it if I have a talent for building these evil things? It's not something I'm proud of!"

I'd heard enough. McCabe was obviously right about Persis. It was time to call for help.

"Q.U.I.P., hit the panic button! We need the police ASAP! Call SE Security, too!"

I waited for my wristwatch to respond but heard only silence. Suddenly, I realized that my right wrist felt sort of naked.

"Looking for this?" Persis asked me. She reached over and lifted something up off the counter. My wristwatch dangled from her fingers. "I've already removed the power cell, but just to play it safe . . ."

She plucked a pen-shaped laser wielder from the counter with her other hand. A bright red beam burned through the back of the watch, incinerating the delicate circuitry inside. Smoke rose from the watch's toasted guts. "So much for your pet AI."

The sight of the laser zapping my watch made me wince. I had to remind myself that Q.U.I.P. didn't really live inside the fried microprocessors. The watch was just an interface device. Q.U.I.P. still existed on the supercomputers back home and elsewhere.

He just couldn't help me right now.

"You never intended to win the Robo Olympics," I realized. "This was just your way to get past all the security." Ever since the very first day of the finals, MechaCrawler had breezed past the metal detectors and security guards. And nobody had suspected Persis for a moment. "You're planning to use your robot to stage some sort of attack."

She patted the spider-bot on its head. "MechaCrawler has plenty of skills, all more important than winning races or scoring baskets." She looked down at McCabe and me. "For one thing, it's much better at security than stupid athletics. I programmed it to immobilize all intruders—and alert me if it ever caught someone."

I wondered why McCabe had broken into MechaCrawler's trailer this morning. Some sort of last-minute search for evidence? Maybe he felt he was running out of time.

Maybe we all were.

"I don't get it," I asked Persis. "What have you been waiting for? The Robo Olympics are almost over."

"Can't you guess?" she challenged me. "Don't you remember who is going to be at the awards ceremony today?"

"Dr. VanderMeer!" I gasped. Suddenly, it all made sense. TRB's real target was the president's chief scientific adviser—and MechaCrawler was the murder weapon. Since there was no other way to smuggle a weapon into the gymnasium where the final ceremony was being held, the robot spider was the perfect assassin!

"Of course!" Persis said. A scary sort of zeal lit up her face. "What better way to counter all this pro-robot propaganda than by having a 'berserk' robot attack Theodora VanderMeer live on national television?

The American public will never trust robots again!"

I think I liked Persis better when she was shy and afraid to make eye contact. "That's crazy!" I argued. "You're actually going to kill someone just to make some sort of stupid point? Have you gone completely mental?"

Slow down, I thought. Maybe it wasn't too late to talk her out of this insane scheme. I forced myself to take a deep breath and talk to her like a friend. "Please, Persis, think about what you're doing. Trust me, you don't want to go through with this!"

She shook her head. "Of course, I don't *want* to hurt anybody. But there's no other way to warn the world about the danger we're in. Every year there are more computers, more robots, and more technology taking over our lives, but nobody seems to care!" She got all choked up as she talked. "We have to do something drastic to get the world's attention, to get people to wake up in time. This is the only way!"

"But you've got it all wrong!" I told her. "Inventing new machines, making new discoveries, is the most human thing there is. It's all about using our brains to make our lives better. You can't turn your back on the future!"

"Be quiet!" she snapped at me. "I don't want your future . . . and neither do my real friends!"

"Forget it, Tom," McCabe said. "You can't reason with a fanatic."

He was probably right, but I still hated the idea that she was really a full-fledged TRB nutcase. Persis had seemed like a nice person, at least the Persis I thought I'd met. But I guess I had never known the real Persis at all.

I remembered the way she had reacted angrily to the anti-robot demonstrators outside SE Headquarters. Guess that was all just an act.

Her own watch chimed. She glanced down at her wrist.

"Almost time for the ceremony," she announced. I realized that I'd been out cold for a couple of hours. "You were decent to me, Tom, back when you thought I was just another misguided young inventor. So I'm just going to leave you and this cop here while I carry out my mission. Someone will find you eventually, I'm sure, but not until it's too late to stop me. By the time you get free, I'll have disappeared. You'll never see me again."

The door to the trailer swung open briefly, just

long enough for MechaCrawler to scuttle out onto the asphalt. Persis got ready to join her robot. "Sorry you have to miss the ceremony, Tom, but don't worry. The TV footage is sure to be all over the air waves tonight. Everyone in the world is going to see it!"

The door slammed shut, leaving McCabe and me alone in the trailer.

Now what?

"You really suspected me of being TRB?" I asked McCabe, while I tried to slip free of steel cables. Unfortunately, I was an inventor, not an escape artist.

"Not really," the FBI agent admitted. "But after the protest outside your dad's headquarters the other afternoon, I started to worry that you were TRB's main target. After all, your family is pretty high on TRB's hate list."

That's why McCabe was tailing the Speedster last night, I realized. He was just trying to protect me. I felt a twinge of guilt at the way Sandy and I had tricked him.

But there were more important things to worry

about at the moment. "You heard what she said. MechaCrawler is going to attack Dr. VanderMeer," I said, struggling against my bonds. "We have to get out of here!"

A chill ran down my spine as I realized that my entire family, not to mention Yo and Bud, were going to be in the gymnasium as well. They were probably wondering what had happened to me. What if the spider-bot hurt someone else in its rampage? Everybody at the gym was a possible victim.

"I'm open to suggestions." McCabe grunted. I could tell he was trying to get free as well but wasn't doing any better than I was. "I don't suppose you have a minichainsaw hidden on you somewhere?"

"Sorry, I think I left that at home today."

There had to be *something* I could use to free us, though. My mind conducted a quick mental inventory of the trailer's contents. I couldn't see the top of the work counter from where I was lying, but I remembered the pen-size laser wielder Persis had used to zap my watch. If only I could get my hands on that . . . !

"Hang on!" I told McCabe. "I have an idea."

I rolled across the floor until my feet were within

reach of the wall beneath the shiny steel counter. Bending my knees, I kicked the wall with all my strength. My hopes soared as I heard various tools and instruments rattle on top of the counter. *That's it!* I thought. *Keep it going!*

My feet slammed into the wall again and again. The impact caused the entire counter to vibrate, but all I cared about was that one laser wielder. I heard something rolling around overhead. Could that be it?

I gave the wall another kick. A slender device, about the size of a ballpoint pen, rolled off the counter and clattered onto the floor. My eyes lit up. This laser was just like the one I had back at my own lab.

Now for the tricky part . . .

The laser had landed several feet away from me. Flopping around like a fish out of water, I worked my way across the floor until it was only a few inches away from my face. My hands were still pinned to my side, so I had to pick it up with my mouth. The laser's metallic casing tasted funny, but so what. If I could pull this off, there might still be a chance to stop MechaCrawler from killing Dr. VanderMeer.

I had operated a laser wielder zillions of times before but never quite like this. Gripping the device firmly between my teeth, I aimed it at the metal coils crossing my chest. My tongue pressed the on switch and an incandescent red beam began to slice through the steel cords. Smoky fumes tickled my nose.

Careful, I thought. My aim slipped and the hot beam stung my skin. I bit down hard on the laser to keep from crying out. The beam swung back toward the cables, which started to come apart one by one. My arms pushed outward against their bonds, making more progress this time. I switched off the laser for a second and put all my strength into freeing my arms. If SwiftBot could lift three hundred pounds in the weight competition, then I should be able to snap through some charred metal cords. I hoped.

My arm muscles strained against the cables. Coiled metal dug into my skin.

Then the cables came apart on one side, freeing my right arm.

Yes! Almost there!

Now that I had a free hand to work with, the rest was easy. The laser sliced through the remaining coils, and I jumped to my feet, leaving a mess of severed cables on the floor. Then I hurriedly freed McCabe.

"Come on!" I said. The awards ceremony had already started. MechaCrawler could strike at any minute. "Every second counts!"

11

Closing Ceremonies

"Hurry!"

I kicked open the door of the trailer and hit the pavement running. My high-tech sneakers carried me across the lot at record speed as I raced to get to the gym in time. Dr. VanderMeer was supposed to present the medals to the robots personally, which would be the perfect moment for MechaCrawler to attack the famous scientist. I just hoped they hadn't gotten to that part of the ceremony yet.

Please, I thought desperately. *Don't let me be too late!*

Glancing back over my shoulder, I saw Luke McCabe lagging behind me. The FBI agent had a cell phone pressed to his cheek and a frustrated expression on his face. "I can't get through to anyone at the gym!"

The jammers, I realized. The electronic devices were blocking the transmission. The committee still didn't want the robots to be operated by remote control, not even while receiving their awards. That would have kind of defeated the point.

There was no way to call ahead and warn anyone. It was up to us now.

Older and less athletic than me, McCabe couldn't keep up, so I left him behind. Within moments, I saw the entrance to the gym in front of me.

"Coming through!" I waved my Robo Olympics pass at the guards as I sped through the metal detectors. At this point, it would take too long to explain the whole complicated murder scheme to the security staff. McCabe could fill them in when he got there, if it wasn't too late by then. "Boy, did I sleep in!"

To my relief, the guards recognized me and let me run by them. Heart pounding, I rushed into the crowded gym.

The scene resembled the opening ceremony six days ago, except that the audience looked twice as large. Once again a temporary stage had been erected at the far end of the gym floor, beneath the basketball hoop. The fiber-optic torch blazed brightly.

Was I in time? My eyes frantically scanned the stage. To my horror, I saw that FugBot, SwiftBot, and RollerBot had already come on stage to receive their medals. The three robots and their inventors were lined up at the front of the dais to provide the best possible photo opportunity for the reporters and news cameras. Gold, silver, and bronze medals were draped around their necks or, in RollerBot's case, her front bumper. With me a no-show, Yo had escorted SwiftBot on her own. I would have some explaining to do to her when this crisis was over, one way or another.

But where was MechaCrawler? I gasped out loud as I spotted the deadly spider-bot crossing the stage toward Theodora VanderMeer. The unsuspecting Nobel Prize winner waited patiently for the robot, holding out the fourth-place medal. If only she knew how much danger she was in!

Mayor Klyde's booming voice blared from the loudspeakers:

"And finally, our fourth-place winners . . . Persis Chadha and MechaCrawler!"

Persis herself walked a few paces behind her robot. Was I the only one who could see how tense she looked?

Dr. VanderMeer was just seconds away from death, and there was no way I could get to the stage on time. There was only one thing left to do.

"SwiftBot!" I shouted at the top of my lungs. My cry echoed across the length of the gym. "Activate hoops routine . . . defense!"

The robot's basketball programming kicked in immediately. He rushed across the stage to block MechaCrawler from going any farther. Dr. Vander-Meer and the other committee members backed away in confusion—especially after jagged spikes suddenly protruded from the spider-bot's multiple limbs!

Persis must have added the concealed spikes sometime after the judge's inspection. No wonder MechaCrawler had performed so poorly in the competitions! It had been designed for a completely different purpose. For a second, I wondered if Persis had picked the spider-design just to amp up the fear factor.

Probably. Who knows? The spikes might have even been tipped with poison.

The spider-bot lunged at Dr. VanderMeer, but SwiftBot jumped between them. The lethal spikes scraped against my robot's silver casing. Every slash struck sparks off SwiftBot's carbon-fiber shell. The clashing metal sounded like a car crash.

Meanwhile, I was sprinting across the floor of the gym, waving my arms to attract everyone's attention. "Run for it!" I yelled at the people on the stage. "That bug's a killer!"

To my surprise, FugBot panicked and shoved Andy aside as the ebony robot bolted from his place in line. He jumped from the stage and ran away from MechaCrawler as fast as his plastic legs could carry him. "Hey, wait for me!" Andy yelled as he chased after his robot. "We've gotta get out of here!"

By now even the audience was lunging from their seats and running for the exits. In the chaos, I glimpsed Persis trying to slip away unnoticed.

Up on the stage, SwiftBot kept playing defense against MechaCrawler. He extended his arms and elbows out to the sides, blocking the spider-bot every chance he got. I was relieved to see Theodora VanderMeer, Mayor Klyde, and the others climb down off the stage behind SwiftBot. Yo and Sue scurried around to join me on the floor, right below the edge of the dais.

"Tom!" Yo exclaimed. "Where have you been? And what's all this craziness about?"

"Yeah!" Sue said. "When did the Robo Olympics turn into BattleBots?"

"I'll explain later!" I promised. "Right now we've got to stop MechaCrawler before it kills someone!"

Sparks flew as the two robots fought on the stage above us. An idea hit me.

"SwiftBot! Execute lift routine!"

Our robot instantly went into weight lifting mode. He grabbed onto MechaCrawler's central thorax and hoisted the killer robot high above his head. The spider-bot's deadly limbs thrashed violently as it tried to break free from SwiftBot's grip. I wasn't sure how much longer he could hold MechaCrawler aloft.

"Get ready!" I warned Sue.

She guessed what I had in mind. "Anytime, dude!"

SwiftBot's arms quivered from the weight of the mechanical spider. MechaCrawler slipped from his fingers and hit the stage hard, landing flat on its back. Its legs flailed helplessly for a moment, then moved to right itself.

"Go, RollerBot!" Sue shouted. "Demolition derby!"

The tanklike robot came to life and ran MechaCrawler over. Her heavy treads crushed the other robot beneath them. The vicious spikes snapped off like they were made out of glass.

"Solid rubber tires," Sue bragged. "One hundred percent puncture-proof!"

RollerBot drove down off her victim, leaving a mass of crumpled metal behind. Air leaked from dozens of ruptured pneumatic cylinders. MechaCrawler sparked and jerked for a second or two before finally breaking down for good. The venomous robot spider looked like a squashed bug. Oil and hydraulic fluid leaked over the stage.

"Eeww!" Yo said, making a face. "I am *not* cleaning that up!"

"Who cares?" Sue said. "We beat that crazy creepy-crawly. Robot teamwork rules!"

And nobody got hurt. That was the important thing.

But what about Persis? Had she gotten away? I climbed up onto the stage and searched the crowds pouring out through the exits. The security crew was trying to keep the evacuation under control, but it was still pretty much a zoo. It wouldn't be hard for Persis to sneak away in the confusion.

Or maybe she already had.

Wait! There she was! Just as I was about to give up, I spotted Persis among the crowd. She was only a few yards away from the exit. A few more moments and she would have made her escape.

"Stop!" I shouted, pointing at the would-be terrorist. "Don't let that girl get away! She's responsible for all of this!"

My yelling attracted some confused looks, but nobody, not even the guards, seemed to catch what I was saying. There was too much else going on. Persis smirked at me as she stepped toward the door . . . and ran right into Luke McCabe.

The FBI agent was panting and out of breath, but that didn't stop him from taking Persis into custody. He flashed his badge at the guards and promptly dragged her away in handcuffs.

Too bad she was such a nutcase. She could have been an awesome inventor.

Bud came running up to us, clutching his notepad and pencil. "Spill, dude! What's the scoop on all the wild robot-versus-robot action?"

"It's a long, twisted story," I said, "but I can tell you what tonight's big headline is going to be: ROBOTS SAVE FAMOUS SCIENTIST FROM TERRORIST PLOT!"

Not exactly what TRB had in mind . . .

"Whoa! Get a load of this!" Yo exclaimed.

Now what?

"I don't believe it," Sue said.

Turning around, I saw Mr. Radnor and a pair of guards escorting Andy and FugBot away from the exits. Andy looked annoyed and embarrassed, but that wasn't the weird part. Jay Robertson's head was sitting atop FugBot's shoulders, while Mr. Radnor held on to what appeared to be FugBot's skull-like head.

I blinked in confusion before I realized what I was seeing: a man in a robot suit.

"Look what we found," Mr. Radnor said. "These guards tried to stop Andy's robot from running away—only to find out he wasn't really a robot at all!"

So *that's* why FugBot had such humanlike reflexes and abilities. He was really a genuine Olympic athlete in disguise. Andy must have presented a genuine robot to the inspectors at the beginning of the games, then pulled a switcheroo later. I was willing to bet Yo a year's worth of pizzas that you'd find another version of FugBot resting in Andy's trailer right now.

"You've hit a new low, Foger," Yo said. "Even for you."

Bud was madly scribbling notes. "Dang, this story just keeps getting better and better!"

Andy glowered back at us. "You're just jealous 'cause you didn't think of it first," he said sullenly.

"Yeah, right!" Sue said sarcastically. "Maybe on Planet Foger."

Compared to Persis's murderous scheme, Andy's scam was a stupid stunt, but it still made me want to punch him in the jaw. Persis at least had the excuse that she was a homicidal fanatic. Andy was just a jerk.

"I can't speak for the committee," Mr. Radnor said, "but I think this almost certainly disqualifies FugBot . . . which changes the rankings somewhat. You know what that means?"

"SwiftBot takes first place!" Yo exclaimed. A stunned expression came over her face. "Tom, we won the grand prize after all!"

"I guess so!" I shook my head in disbelief. "How awesome is that?"

"With RollerBot coming in second," Mr. Radnor added. "As soon as the judges can make it official."

"What else can they do?" Sue reached out and shook my hand, then Yo's. "Let me be the first to congratulate you on your glorious victory." She gave us a crafty smile. "And just wait until next year!"

"You're on!" I told her. "I can hardly wait."

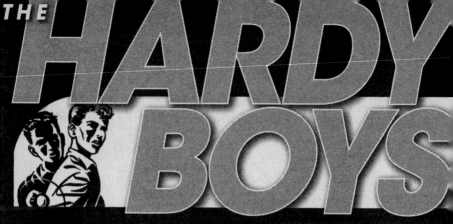
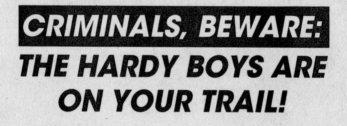

PENDRAGON

Bobby Pendragon is a seemingly normal fourteen-year-old boy. He has a family, a home, and a possible new girlfriend. But something happens to Bobby that changes his life forever.

HE IS CHOSEN TO DETERMINE THE COURSE OF HUMAN EXISTENCE.

Pulled away from the comfort of his family and suburban home, Bobby is launched into the middle of an immense, interdimensional conflict involving racial tensions, threatened ecosystems, and more. It's a journey of danger and discovery for Bobby, and his success or failure will do nothing less than determine the fate of the world. . . .

PENDRAGON

by D. J. MacHale

Book One: The Merchant of Death
Book Two: The Lost City of Faar
Book Three: The Never War
Book Four: The Reality Bug
Book Five: Black Water

Coming Soon: Book Six: The Rivers of Zadaa

From Aladdin Paperbacks • Published by Simon & Schuster